04/22

D1246663

RUSSIAN LOVER

Russian Lover

& other stories

JANA MARTIN

yeti

YETI books are published by Verse Chorus Press in association with YETI. Verse Chorus Press, PO Box 14806, Portland OR 97293. yetipubs@gmail.com.

The characters and events in this book are fictitious. Any similarity to real persons, living or dead, is coincidental and not intended by the author.

"Work" originally appeared in *Chronogram*; "Galletas" in *Five Points*; "Hope" in *Glimmer Train*; "Russian Lover" and "Why I Got Fired" in *Spork*; "Perforation: a Lexicon," "I'm Not Quite Finished Yet," and "Try" on sporkpress.com; "Tremor" and "The Father" in *Turnstile*; "Belmar" in *Willow Springs*; "Factory" in *Yeti* and on sporkpress.com; "Goodbye John Denver" in *Yeti*; and "Rubber Days" in *Yeti* and (in an earlier form) in *Pretty Decorating*.

Cover painting © Steve Sas Schwartz [*www.sasart.com*]
Cover design: Patricia Fabricant
Book design: Steve Connell

FIRST EDITION

Printed in Canada

Library of Congress Cataloging-in-Publication Data

Martin, Jana.
    Russian lover & other stories / Jana Martin. -- 1st ed.
      p. cm.
    ISBN 978-1-891241-52-9
    I. Title. II. Title: Russian lover and other stories.
    PS3613.A7795R87 2007
    813'.6--dc22

                                    2007000438

CONTENTS

Thanks to Mike McGonigal and Steve Connell of Yeti, to Evelyn McDonnell and Vivien Goldman, to Joy Williams, Janice Eidus, Elizabeth Evans, Jane Miller and Diane Vreuls, to Elaina Ganim, Tedra Meyer, Carolanne Patterson and Deena Mitchell, to Megan Sexton, Drew Burk, Richard Siken and Phillip Levine, to Nancy Martin, Ted Shaw, Michael P. Nordberg, N. Knight, D.B., Barbara Lesch-McCaffrey and Michael McCaffrey, Kitty and the women of Flavor Cage. Thanks also to the Mink Hollow Arts Committee, the Olderbark Endowment, and Safe Mountain SAR.

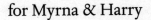

for Myrna & Harry

HOPE

It's been four red-eyed hours from Boston to the Port Authority, New York. A family caught my eye as I wobbled down the aisles, thinking movement might be good, and what a mistake that was. The movement, I mean. On one side of the grimy aisle fidgeted two dirty-nosed boys with their fists clutched around their mother's dark and heavy hair. And right across the aisle but a whole gully away sat their father, irritably trying to read a Sanskrit newspaper—words scrolling down in blue and red lines. What I looked like in the sallow buslight I don't even want to know, but now we've parked at the terminal and they've spotted me here at the newsstand filching mints, and they think we're friends.

In five minutes we all board the bus bound for Florida, a northeast transfer, as the loudspeaker says. And here's the family waving their tawny, boneless waves in this hideous air, and I think, what am I doing, if only for a moment. Lifesavers in my hand, I am completely trapped into feeling like this bus ride, this migration south, is the wrong thing.

"Young lady," the father calls in a deep, spicy voice. "Do you know what time our next bus is scheduled to leave?" Like the waiter bowing, *you would like more tea*, at Punjab, that restaurant I used to go to, back when the Boyfriend was good and I was good. And even just standing here, palming the Lifesavers and thinking that—oh, the backstab of memory—I know this is not the wrong thing. This northeast transfer to a southeast-heading bus, it may not be right. But at this point may I just think and may I just say that there is also no wrong?

This bus is dark and dirty, is woolly and stickyfloored, and me and my jumblehead have taken up the backseat again. There's a guy in front of me with a strange bluish cast to his teeth, and I think he's going to be a problem. He keeps peering over the seat or between the crack, smiling and starting to say something. I sniff and look somewhere deliberately, and he looks there and can't figure out what I'm looking at, which makes him feel dumb, so he decides not to talk.

Fine. Really. Fine with me.

This next endless leg, I thought, and about this was wrong, would be on a superior rather than inferior bus, since it's a thirty-nine-hour ride with stops everywhere. Even between Boston and New York there were strange and pointless stops where the driver just got out and left. In Connecticut he pulled into a service station that was closed, but he went inside anyway. Ten minutes, maybe, before he came out, wiping his mouth. All business and burp as he took his mashed-down seat. This second driver is a spread of jowl and gut at the wheel, taking us all with a lurch out onto the road, but what a relief of motion—we pass cars, the swish of airstreams between vehicles whisper, Unwrong, unwrong.

What I left in Boston was a gone-bad me, a gone-bad boyfriend, November's bastard cold whistling through our apartment—more like apart. Always the bad landlord whistling "Cara Mia" all day instead of fixing the heat like he said. I bruised myself at night by bumping into the wall in my sleep, my skin too cold to be resilient, blood too confused by all the chemicals pumped in: What did you say my job was? Could you tell me again? I'm just a little spaced out—Bad no-touch thing. I couldn't, I can't be touched. It hurts, almost. Not an actual hurt but a tickling, nagging, just-can't-take-it kind of hurt. Even a hand on my back made my insides jump.

Boyfriend? A pseudo rocker in smallbutt jeans, had no sense of loyalty, did it with girls from the junior high down the street and then stole their buspasses, their lunches, and from me stole anything. Stole the wool socks my father sent, my well-meaning sweetheart father who lives in a past of fountain pens and correspondence and buttondowns. My father who'd pinned a letter to the socks:

> Just concerned that in light of the bad economy,
> which has been the focus of all the papers, my
> daughter's developing the bad habit of being
> discouraged, and I would urge you to reject

unemployment for the satisfaction of an honest
wage, if a minimum wage at that.

If he really knew what was going on, he'd be speechless.
He'd be red. He'd be non-erudite, stammeringly mad. But I
don't want to talk about it. In the bus is someone sneaking a
joint nearby. Sucking sounds, airless voices as they talk through
the toke. They probably wish they had the backseat and think
I'm a hog: I'm one small girl with a ratty Irish face to them. But
I've escaped the bad stuff after all. Soon I will be a girl on the
peninsula, the arm of the country, down somewhere near the
index finger if you look at Florida that way. I'll eat in cafeterias
and live in a motel room for eighteen a night. I wanted to show
Dad the map, wanted to tell him my plans and show him the
suitcase I found to pack in. But with these arms of mine, not a
chance.

But haven't I escaped by way of my arm in actual medical
fact? My arm became an emergency one night last week, when
a microspeck of dirt like some impure thought hitched a ride
on the needle's shaft as it went in. And my arm went No, and
swelled like an overboiled hot dog, those plump-when-you-
cook-'em kind, and twenty-four hours later that limb was bilious, outraged, filled with yellow infuriation. The emergency
room was scowling faces, a mean-lipped stitcher giving me the
"You are perfectly qualified for insurance" lecture, meaning
You're a white girl—what the hell are you living off our social
programs for? A rustle-legged nurse recited, "Need we inform
you that cleanliness of the wound is your responsibility," as I

throbbed, as her pantyhosed legs rubbed against each other and she circled me, while the betadine rivered orange over my final narcotic offense.

Yes, I decided sitting among the whitecoats, from now I will refuse anything stronger than percoset, though I had to argue with them to get some. "But you have no idea," I managed to say, "what a step this is, for me, in the right direction." Talking to walls over there, don't ask the system why it does what it does. It has nothing to do with gifts or love, nothing to do with anything but clipboards, paperwork, the quantity in the supply closet—just make sure there's some left over for the staff.

Me that night, clutching the little manila pill envelope and talking to Dad from the payphone on Boylston Street instead of going to see him. Me too pale and bandaged up, and while my voice could hide it, my face couldn't. Can't fake it visually when I'm that punctured. This way he could ask, "How are you?" and mean it, and I could tell him in a way that mattered. So I said, "Dad. I'm tired of this Boston thing, tired of every-thing. It's too cold. I need to retire. I need rest and sun."

Picture my father at the kitchen table, my father at his black rotary phone by the can of Quaker Oats. I see it all the time, the place I'll miss the most. My out-of-it father who's more in it than anyone, so sweet to all these dastardly souls that it breaks my heart.

We have a little thing going, me and Dad. A joke thing. "If you want to retire, why not try Florida?" he said, mimicking a travel agent advising a geriatric. He was making a little joke so I could say, "Kidding," right away. We take turns at this: I make a joke, he takes it literally. "Go take a hike," I ribbed him once, and he said, "Great idea!" and got his boots. But advice is another thing. Taken, at least by me, as a joke. We only speak the same language sometimes. So on the payphone, as Saabs bumped over T tracks and overcoats flapped in the wind, I said, "You're right, Dad. You're absolutely right."

"Get a bus ticket," he said, still joking. "I'll reimburse you when my ship comes in."

How very retro and endearing and tragic. The bus station was so near the hospital; did they do that on purpose? My last hours in Beantown I wandered the cold dawn, scanning the discards put out for Mafia trash trucks. In Back Bay I found an old suitcase nicely propped against a frozen tree. It was what my dad would call a two-suiter, but it was more like a lady's case, which my dad would call a two-nighter—

I mean why is it that the men's stuff is known by what you put in it, and the women's by how long you go for?

This suitcase was pale blue satin inside, a little moldy, a little crushed. But still it gave off a scent, like lavender and boiled potatoes. Like Irish sisters, never married. The name on the tag was written in a parlor hand: O'Toole. Perhaps the secret spinster branch of that famous actor's family, the shadowy figures haunting tall Peter O'Toole? What gave him the darklined eyes and his face's sad creases, indelible despite all the orange juice and swimsuit dealings in Hollywood.

These percoset associations go slow. The bus gears shift on a downhill. Someone's eating chocolate in here; I can smell the wrapper and the nuts.

Standing in the kitchen doorway, smallbutt Boyfriend watched me take the applesauce jar of money out of the oven. The oven was our bank; of course we never cooked. The morning's pinkish light seeped through the blinds, flattering him just a little. "Where you going?" he said like it was a big surprise. "You coming back? Where's the suitcase from? Would be great for my records." He was mumbling, eye focused on some oblique summary of a story still forming. "Get anything from the hospital? Pills? Codeine? Leave the money, right?"

Oh no, I thought. I protect my own. From now on, I protect my own as a father wants to protect his own daughter.

Six or seven hours since New York and are we anywhere? We're in the dark. It's an aquarium out there and we're a lone fish in the giant tank, a tank gone uncleaned forever, stuck in the basement of the Natural History Museum no one goes to anymore. Another minor but sad change to this world, my father would say. The smells in the rear of this bus sweep me back to parochial school, cauliflower boiling in lunchroom pots, the nuns' coffee breath: consume without pleasure, it's so much better for the trip Upstairs. I smell like sweat off a zoo animal. It's good to be next to the bathroom. I'll be sick the next thirty or forty hours so I might as well be hopping distance. The routine is: cramp, run to the can, be sick, sit there exhausted, drag myself back to my seat, slump against the upholstery, cramp, run to the can.

I get to be the misfit rider on this bus, the passenger everyone wishes would get off at the rest stop and forget to get back on. Wouldn't they love to watch me baffled and dazed, the wretch chasing the taillights and waving while no one on the bus says a word? Well, I apologize for my acrid funk, but it would take more than walking down three rubbertread steps to get lost right now. I mean I'm already lost, already dazed. I mean the purple and red seat in front of me is an eel-and-spigot-patterned factory weave, and that man in front of me is turning around. The air is beyond stale. We're lungs struggling over the same air we struggled over hours ago. I want a cool breeze. Even a picture of a cool breeze. Blue ocean and an umbrella drink and slender fingers on the straw. So cruel, really, to bestow only eight Lifesavers per pack.

Richmond, Virginia and I'm already down those three steps before the driver says, "Miss, we haven't come to a full stop yet. Will you please re-ascend and place your feet behind the yellow line—"

Why does everyone official throw all their officialese at me, and why does he bother saying the line is yellow since in this light, like everything else, it's white? When he says "yet" it comes out more like "yit," which comes out like a racial slur—Hey, you stupid yit, welcome to my bus, now get off and go back where you and your smell came from, and don't even think about looking for a better life.

But the airbrakes finally fart: we're no longer moving. There's that special I-refuse-to-look-at-you from the driver, who's staring through his giant windshield like he's facing deep space from the Starship Enterprise. Like I refuse to look at you so therefore you are not there. Last step down, then I slide through a streak of southern mud. Like soup. Bad associations for sick me.

This rest stop is dinging pinball machines and white butts spilling out of bluejeans at the counter. I am sour. My teeth feel scraped. The passengers wander through the gift shop aisles and disappear. I hear a cat meowing in that ass-in-the-air, belly-scraping-ground way. But there's no sign of a cat in here. No sign of a crouching female beggar, whiskers after any fellow she can find. Unstoppable, though, that yowling. Reminds me, terribly, of Boyfriend and junior-high-school knees, strange bookbags thrown on top of my clothes. So I decide to call Dad. There's always the chance he'll say, You're where? I didn't mean that.

Then what? His daughter's descending the country in a bus. There's always the chance he'll be angry, as in, I'm disappointed. You could at least have come in person to say goodbye. And then, the chance of suspicion. As in, Who are you with? Why didn't you come to see me? Then the obvious: What happened to you?

But to ask that would not mean he wanted the answer. And this, for some reason, makes my eyes well up, makes me cramp and curl in on myself: I grab a magazine rack for balance. The body agrees with the mind, occasionally. And we're supposed to feel good about that.

My luck is that there's a phone booth down the aisle, so I can close the door and be alone. My luck is that there's a man in the phone booth. He's bigger than he should be and he's closed the door anyway. He looks like he just had a double stack with a side of sausage and sunnyside-up soft, two cups black, bring me home-fries. My luck is that he now appears to be arguing and working up a post-digestive sweat—

My luck is that he slams the receiver and wrenches open the door, and doesn't apologize when he knocks into my shoulder, stomping his way back to cup number three of black, a cruller for dessert.

He was, while in this cubicle, this public cubicle, redolent. The air is slurry. The receiver's slurry. Plastic, they say, can never really be cleaned. You have to abrade it. Which is what they suggested, in the emergency room, I do to my arm once I'm ready to look for a job. I didn't understand it at first—thought they were suggesting I braid my arm. Like hair. They corrected me. "A-brade," they enunciated. They stretched out my right arm and ran a gloved finger over the bad spots. I flinched. "Unlike the pain you already put yourself through," they said, "this pain will be worth something."

No discounts on that kind of logic.

Phone-booth door cracked for oxygen's sake, piped-in country music seeps into this tiny chamber with it. My luck is that my father says, "From who?" to the operator's drawl: she made my name sound more like Hole than Hope. At the last moment, when she's about to disconnect, he says, "Oh. Yes. I'll accept."

"Dad," I say. "I took your advice. I'm really on my way to Florida. I'm on the bus."

I expected, like I said, this kind of silence. There's a cello and piano thing going on in the background. Very dignified and Bostonian.

"Dad? Don't be mad. I really meant it. About retiring. I've lived so fast. I mean you can only move through life at a certain speed without needing to stop for a rest."

Dad?

I can see him, sitting by the rotary phone, its heavy receiver a familiar weight in his hand. He's perhaps in the middle of a snack of cheddar cheese, apples, tea. He's perhaps in slippers. He has kept up the rudiments of life's daily ebbs and flows. He is unsure, perhaps, of what he's hearing. He has perhaps gotten up from a nap to answer the phone. He naps, sometimes, flat on his back on the bed. A disturbing position to view from the position of a young woman burning with life in the doorway. My feet, I notice now, are cold, the toes numb—I wish I had those wool socks. As I think that, perhaps he is thinking this: My daughter is aging me, right now.

"Dad. Talk to me. I got the ticket and I'm just headed south for a little while to warm up. I'm on my way. It feels good. How are you?"

"Well," he says. "I can't say that I am used to your acting on the advice bestowed upon you. I can't say that."

"I thought it was great advice," I say. "Even if you were kidding around."

"Can't say you've ever acted on the advice bestowed upon you when I wasn't kidding around."

"Just think of it this way, Dad. Regardless of the method, it worked."

"I suppose." His voice trails off. I'm the good daughter, reeling him back.

"I'm in a rest stop, Dad. It's full of people."

"And what is your scheduled arrival?"

"A few days? I'm not sure."

"And is it comfortable? And relaxing?"

"Leave the driving to us, as they say."

"Then it sounds like a good idea," he says. "You'll get some color on your face, which will be nice for when you're back here."

I don't really understand that, but he's probably thinking of the hikers we saw at the arboretum last month: youthful, vigorous people with apple cheeks and heavy sweaters. Which can make you feel so . . . unhealthy.

"You think you need a break. I need to retire for good," he says wearily.

"I'll send you the ticket," I joke.

We're back in our usual mode, and his laugh says, All's well with the world after all, so I'll just hang up on this happy note. He's such a good fellow, such a pat-on-the-back kind of man, it's heartbreaking. My modestly witty father in his undershirts and trousers, the failed filmmaker turned projectionist, my mother always a picture burning up the film. He was running a camera at a Cambridge art house the night she left. Showing, he'd say later, *La Dolce Vita*. She called him up to say goodbye and caught him in the middle of changing reels, and he never quite recovered. He was so shocked he forgot to start the motor, left the projector stalled. The projector lamp burned a hole into one frame and the whole theater watched that one picture catch on fire, I mean 280, 241, 284, maybe 248, or close to 284 people in there—

But it's not pity I'm after. It's hope. I'm not wallowing. I'm merely recollecting. For those of us who are born into this kind of world, we live in this kind of world. Do not think we dwell on it. We just tell these stories instead of other stories. Instead of the kind where dotty Aunt Gert came for Thanksgiving and forgot to turn the oven on to cook the turkey, or where we are all headed north for a summer vacation and Dad took a wrong turn and drove the Dodge right into a pond in the dark—

There's strawberry jam in the treads of the floor. It's not red but smells sweet and reminds me not of jam, but peanut butter. Since I hate grape jelly, I've always requested strawberry and someone on this bus at some point—not on this trip but another trip, a recent one to who knows where—someone out there agrees with me about strawberry jam. Against the rubber this patch of jam takes on a faint sheen in a kind of lace pattern, and perhaps if you could scrape off the layers of shoe dirt there'd be that perfect red underneath. A perfect red spot teeming with microactivity. Healthy, rusharound cells. I've gone through nearly all the money in the applesauce jar, between the one hundred and something dollars for the one-way ticket and the assorted snacks in Richmond. And that guy sitting in front of me, the one with the teeth, has woken up again, and is playing that just-about-to-speak game—

Which means I have to play the just-about-to-ignore-your-existence game, which means a split-second turn of my head to a faraway point he can't see, which turns out to be the luggage rack above the seats across the aisle, where there is an open bag of white bread, and slices jostle out of the bag, one at a time—

"Hum," the man's just said. So he's probably undaunted this time, bold from being cooped up, renewed from sleeping. Maybe I've got a few minutes before he starts, and as the bus bumps over the road the slices cascade, and I've never stared at falling white bread harder—

The second time my dad drove into a pond in the dark, he did it on purpose. He was also headed on vacation, but the kind of vacation you don't return from. Bitterly disappointed because the pond was a shallow puddle of muck instead of a lake, he ruined the car but not his life, just set himself back, ashamed and car-less. "After all," he'd say while waiting for the insurance man to call him back, my father sitting by the rotary phone in the kitchen, its black face with that circle of little circles, all numbered and lettered with the predigital efficiency of a kinder, paper-based time. "It was a good car. I may have erred in judgment, but I could still use the car. After all, it got me where I needed to go."

And I'd say, to make a little joke in our dry way, "If that's where you want to go."

How I knew he was low? Instead of humor he just saw the tragedy. "It's hopeless," he said, stabbing the columns of insurance costs with his pencil stub. "I'm not meant to be dramatic. I'll leave the fancy exits to your mother and you."

Legacy, I'm thinking, on the can again in the bus bathroom. I
mean here I am. There's a woman in a wig waiting for me outside. She knocked a minute ago, then just opened the door and
stood there, squinting through marvelous green eyeglasses.
She said, "You a girl or a boy?"

Here come the stampeding issues of hygiene. Were I a boy,
would she feel reduced to using what might as well be a urinal?
Or would she feel relieved to know I'm a girl, and she's once
again escaped male filth? This is not my father's idea of fancy.
I hope he never finds out about this—the arm of it, you could
say. Or the vein of it. The damp armpit of it, adding its funk to
the whole gang of scents in the unmoving air.

The woman's lips are coral colored, a lifeless gloss that adds
to my gut cramp. She held the door open while I took a second
to think of an answer. Girl or boy? I thought of Boston, the
writhing nights. I have friends that could tweak her worldview
with a garter snap: sex doesn't always make you know what
you are. Her voice crawled inside the dirty cup of my ear. She
could've asked, You take baths or showers? Same difference, I
would have said. My hair's short from getting singed on the
stove, then hacked off. I was too gone to light my cigarette
with a match so I leaned over the burner, then went nuts with a
scissors trying to cut out the melts, lightbulb filaments clinking
in the bulb.

"Guess," I said to the lady.

She said, "Only girls make people guess. So you're that,
right?"

Why answer the inquiries of unanswerable people? Why

look her square in the eyes with a mouth full of sallow taste and a gut full of cramp? My father, condemned to be a good man, might enjoy this moment for its comedy, if he could view it from a distance, which is the only way I'd ever want him to see it.

"Haven't checked lately," I said to her. "But I think I need to continue with this?"

She realized she was addressing someone with their pants down and as I fumbled with the roll of paper, she ducked back and slammed the door. I've never so treasured the privacy of two square feet of space, gently rocking as the bus covers the road. But she's still there, I know. I can hear her shoes, sticking to the patch of jam.

In Brunswick, Georgia, the man sitting in front of me gets up his guff again. Here it comes. I'm sweating a pickle smell. His arm is pressing so hard into the bus seat that the cushion bawls like a calf. "Hey," he says in a too-bright voice. "Here's a question. What would you do if you were on a beach, say Miami Beach—"

"I've never been there," I say. "That's why I'm going."

"Well, just wait. Just say you're at any beach. They're all this way. Debris washing up. Flotsam and jetsam. Probably more sam, right? I mean, Sam? I mean beaches these days, right? Some people will do just about anything on a beach."

"All right," I say, not wanting to get involved, and knowing the quickest way to end this is to cooperate. "I'm with you."

"You're walking," he starts, "and you find a used condom in

the sand."

"What?"

"You're walking, and you find a used rubber. A prophy-lactic."

"I know what they are."

"Well you've just found one on the beach."

"Don't people usually bury them?"

"Hey, I'm working out a theory here, so can I finish?"

"Sure," I say.

"I mean there's something about it, see?"

"Ugh." I feel like acting the prude. My father would like that.

"No. I mean yes. Of course. But think. Consider this. There's something about it. It's got something in it."

"Sure does," I say.

"No. Wait. See you look at it, and you realize there's some-thing inside it that looks kind of like money. You realize it's got money in it. A bill."

"Not a chance," I say. "How did it get there?"

"A fifty-dollar bill in it. You can see the numbers—Five. O."

"Impossible," I say.

"No, really. It's got a big bill inside it. You don't have any idea why. But there it is. Fifty smackeroos. Now. What do you do?"

"Oh," I say. "That's a hard one."

"Well it was," he laughs, "but probably not anymore. Anyway, what? Would you try to get it? Would you stick your

fingers in there? Would you stick something else in there?
Would you risk it?"

"That's a tough one," I say, stalling. He's happy that he's got
my attention. He's happy that he's made me think. I wonder
how long it took him to come up with the question. Maybe
he rides buses days and nights and just thinks up things to ask
people, feeling like he's some sort of Grand Unsettler, his purpose in life being to shake out the truth. Maybe he heard the
whole story in a bar. His eyes have that glint of someone who
knows his question to be perfect and unanswerable. For him,
I put a stumped look on my face. But I can only think of one
answer, the only answer I really have.

See, safety is not really an issue for me anymore. It's kind
of a non-issue. It's a one-way wall climbed over. I can't climb
back. It's gloves on everyone's hands when they have to touch
me, sooner or later.

"Well," I say. "It's too late for me. It really is."

"Right," he says.

"I mean it. It wouldn't matter."

There's a pause as my heart slows down and his heart
speeds up. I know this. I've expected this. I mean, I haven't told
anyone, but I knew this is the way it would be.

"Hey," he says, graven now, his bluish teeth ducking inside
his dry lips. He settles back into his seat. "The fact has been
recorded," he says quietly. "I hear you, lady. Loud and clear.
Ten-four. I hear you."

His apology is kind of soothing—"And I'm sorry, I really
am sorry"—over and over, until I'm on the brink of sleep.

He was the only one I would ever tell, I decided as my arm heated up. I pressed my cheek against the cool of the dark window for a distraction. Then I took the rest of the percosets so I wouldn't scratch. Scratching is life, though, isn't it? So I scratched. Then I was sure I was making indelible marks. I scratched because I was worried, then wished it were light so I could see if I had reason to worry. Not the overhead light, which I would've clicked on if I could disengage my nails from my arm long enough to reach up. Not that light. What a garish sight that might be, my battle-scarred arm in the reading light. Read bad shape, read mess, read old betadine. But if light filtered in from the outside, I decided, if it streamed in with the new day, I'd take that. I could look at nearly anything in that light.

Outside it was still dark and the bus still rumbled along. But there was a very slight cast to the outside, not even a color, just a lifting of the heaviest layer of dark. And still inside was all stale air and too-long sitting, all of us in here. The clumsy whisper sounds of heavy people shifting in the seats, the creak of the undercarriage, a baby letting out one cry, those children with their mother, pestering, "Why can't we get off your lap, why can't we get off the bus?" their hands yanking into her hair.

Finally it's Orlando, and orange groves and horse farms. The bus takes me down this coast, traveling away from the freezing rain, the puritan looks on the T. I'm an escapee descending into nitrate canals, green lawns, unnameable birdflocks, the rays of new sun. In the lull of wheels and transmission shift and the slight seepage of carbon monoxide from the engine, just enough to soothe, I have made a list of all the jobs I am willing to take.

Waitress, pet-shop clerk, cage cleaner at a zoo, lunchbag stuffer for bad children at a center, ticket-taker at movies—sullen but glamorous in a dingy booth. There are so many wonderful things to do if only you imagine yourself a neophyte starlet, doe-eyed and ignorant of your own past twenty years. To have such little dreams takes serious revision, takes serious No, Dad, just let me get somewhere first and then I'll get somewhere beyond it.

I will jerk orange juice into cone cups at a drugstore. I will dust off boxes of envelopes in the five-and-dime. I will time dental X-rays. I will rotate the chickens roasting on the supermarket rotisserie for the retirees to buy, so they can gum the soft meat and get some protein, which everybody needs.

My father will be proud of me. He will forget his tragic years and he will not be interested in the ways I have failed. He will not pry. He will just be proud of his blood and the way he upbrought me.

And me, when I land, I will not think of my father in the muck-pond, tragically averting his own end, or those wool socks stretched by thieving feet, or the pant-less girls nodding out on my bed, Boyfriend looking at them puzzled, asking me, Can you get rid of her? I mean, I will remember. But there will be something else, more simply spelled out and drawn in brighter colors, like a primer on how to grow up, with words like food, house, money, job. We're taught well, don't you see, when we're still young. Think of those black-lettered words next to the happy pictures. If we only knew how to obey them. See Spot run. See Hope try.

We're ready to live our way right out of kindergarten. But we have to wait for everyone else to step aside, and don't you know it, they don't always. Or they step aside so far that they land in an entirely different country, and how can you take their place? I'm not making excuses. I'm not blaming bad Boyfriend, or the tancoat down the street with his little dimebags of boric mindsquawk, and certainly not my father, alone with the quartet, as I crawled up the calico wallpaper in my Massachusetts bedroom.

Here I am, a girl on a bus. My eyes are getting used to this subtropical glare, this mega-light. Oh, what a diet this light must be. The trees whoosh with joy and rattle their fronds at the sky. White birds have tracked us for miles now, attracted to the bus's silver back. Here you can appreciate the shape of buses, their long, shiny sweep of brilliant tin, that running dog on the side stretching his legs far as he can. I am heading for the land of smocks and weekly wages, for the land of swimming pools. I am heading for the land of paper bags for kids with sunburned noses and grubby hands.

My father, I'm sure, will make up a nice story about me. She is on her way to a teaching certificate. She is learning how to run a nursery school. She was always fond of children, my daughter. Always understood them, she felt. Good man. My father, the cardigan innocent, sustained on Quaker Oats.

Looking at the orange groves, the grazing horses, the snug buildings and little people here and there, the floral, chemical scents leaking through the vents, I vow to find my father a sweet wife. That's what he needs. It's been long enough. I don't know if I'll ever want the icy air again, or if I'll miss that bleak northern city. And my father, he needs someone. A woman rooted so tightly to the earth that her way of being upset is to make a giant ham, stick pineapple rings on its sides like big bug eyes, and to weep like a collie over the glaze.

GOODBYE JOHN DENVER

When you have the syndrome you worry and worry
so adrenaline loses patience and beats up your regular chauffeur
gets behind the wheel of your car
and adrenaline has a lead foot,
does not know the meaning of
slow down, slow down, slow down

—The Shrills, "Adrenaline" (1997)

Late one blustery October morning Carl and Rita sat in their old Toyota down at the base of Bridge Street, on their way to Manhattan for a breakfast they didn't want to go to, didn't want to spend $12.95 for overdone eggs in hipsterville. But they had to, Rita said, they had to see her old friend Junie, who they'd stopped seeing ever since Junie's new boyfriend whispered some switcheroo proposition into Carl's ear. And Carl had the idiotic lack of sense, Rita later railed, to tell the guy he'd see what Rita thought.

"Can we not bring it up?" Carl said.

These were two people who loved each other not practically but madly, and felt like two troops in a misfit indie army of scattertag bands that tried to play in the city, sometimes felt glamorous, sometimes beaten down. Carl with a day job, Rita taking a break from temping, from discount-store suits she'd pretend to be Gal Friday in. He was pale, slender, not tall, not short, with coathanger shoulders and a serious but boyish milky face. She was retro fleshpot, cinched into vintage, black lacquered hair, black nails, dark voice. They lived in a shitty loft, drove an old car, maybe someday they'd get married, maybe they'd stay underground forever.

A fleet of garbage trucks from the place behind their building rumbled by, shaking the thin skin of street over the infrastructure.

Rita said, "You thought it was funny, Junie's creepy guy asking that. Next time just say No." She watched a sooty-looking pigeon fly low across the hood of their car to root in the trash that the night winds had gathered on the sidewalks. The wind from the East River was relentless, made October seem November, had muscled a herd of cardboard barrels into the street, which Carl now steered around.

"Next jalopy I want power steering," he said. Since Rita he'd taken to using funny words. She was a collector of the oddest phrases, always coming out with some zinger he'd never heard. Her lyrics were acidic, floral, sick. But sometimes she was straight, brick-heavy.

"And she's still with him," Rita said, one-tracking it.

"Maybe Junie's into it," Carl said, hauling the Toyota around a sudden line of double-parked cars. "Do we really have to go? Can't we renege?" He pronounced it with a soft g.

"It's not like ménage," she said.

"Ménage," he said, drawing the sounds out deliciously.

Rita said, "Junie introduced you and me, and she's invited us to breakfast like six times, and we never go. We have to go."

They continued driving up the hill of Bridge Street, the four blocks toward the Brooklyn-side entrance of the Brooklyn Bridge. They got to the Jay Street intersection, sat at the long light. Carl said, "Some people just have a strange need for indiscretion."

Rita said, "Indiscretion my ass."

Carl said, "Your ass has a lot to do with it."

Rita said, "Can you please not talk about sex?"

"I don't know if I can help talking about sex," Carl said. "What's with this light?"

"Just not so all the time and fourteen about it," Rita said. "Just not breaking into a cold sweat before some skinny Japanese girl in thigh-hi's."

"She's hot," Carl said.

"You know I have enormous respect for the femerotic," Rita said.

"Femerotic," Carl repeated, maneuvering into the rightmost lane. He wanted to avoid being squeezed by anyone else turning right onto the bridge at the last minute. People did that. New York drivers.

"No sex talk at breakfast," she said, "or I won't be able to eat."

Meanwhile, heading east on Gold Street was this kid driving his Dad's blue Pontiac, this kid in a rush at twenty-one and panicked cause he was stuck among the idiots on that stretch of city blocks off the BQE. He hated that part of Gold Street, called it an aberration, a buzz-kill, it was a three-block wincing crawl of city street just because the city couldn't get its shit together to connect the two ends of the highway, so fucking annoying. And so fucking annoying that his father's car didn't have enough pickup to catch all the green lights and so he floored it and braked, floored it and braked, heading towards Bridge Street, which if he timed it right meant he could probably make the entire hook-turn back onto the BQE in one light if he went fast enough.

And Rita and Carl sat in their car like dumb sheep with funny-colored hair, and crossed Jay Street and moved up the hill, and Rita went on about how their neighborhood, this neighborhood, was just an industrial nowhereland crossed with streets named after not even dignitaries, just people on the take. Cheap lawyers, she decided: Jay, Gold, she could imagine an entire firm of fierce little men scurrying about, a middling little firm with an appetite for dirty fights. And mostly you only knew these streets as ways to get somewhere more important or populated, one of those places people only went to go somewhere else.

"You know Junie's creep is a lawyer," Carl said. And the light for Gold Street was going to turn green and Rita said, because they were actually picking up speed, going over ten miles an hour now, "maybe we'll have enough time to do some other stuff, pick up guitar strings, buy some organic groceries, some hair dye." They'd make breakfast quick, and get cigars afterwards and at this bright prospect, Rita clapped her hands. And after Gold Street it was always smooth sailing that last stretch onto the bridge, and as they reached the intersection Rita said, "You know I love cigars, it's so '20s, so—"

And Carl was about to say so femerotic when, perpendicular to them, the kid in the Pontiac smacked the steering wheel and said this is bullshit, there's no one in the intersection anyway, and floored the Pontiac feeling all Indy 500 and shot forward past all those cars next to him that were stopped for the red light like idiots—What you all stopped for well fuck it I'm *going*

and slammed right into the side of Carl and Rita's Toyota.

Actually right behind the door, on Rita's side.

The impact hit the chassis in its funny bone, cracked the front axle like a wishbone and spun the old car about 450 degrees. When it stopped, it was facing back down Bridge Street. They sat there, little globs of window glass slowly falling onto Rita's lap. Rita couldn't quite turn her head. It seemed stuck to the roof of the car.

Rita let her eyes cross to the left to see what Carl was doing. He was sitting foursquare, hands on the wheel, both feet on the floor, staring straight ahead, eyes wide, wide open. She said, "Now I know why they say white knuckled."

Carl said, "You're alive. I can't get my hands to ungrip the wheel. I should pull up the emergency brake."

He did that. They heard metal scrape asphalt underneath them.

A blue Pontiac parked at the curb, a kid in a windbreaker stepped out, lit a cigarette. He looked in their direction, then leaned over and punched his thigh with his fist, whirled around and karate-kicked the Pontiac in the flank.

"Motherfucker," Carl said.

Time spread wide and gray and filled itself with watery light and they sat there inside the busted car. They could feel the day fold into itself, and their plans and chores tumble down into a long, empty shaft. A soundtrack was playing, the screech and crunch of metal, over and over, in Rita's head. She worked her jaw, ran her tongue over her teeth. It was all there. There was a chance they weren't hurt.

There was a siren, a squad car pulled up with two cops, very young, one heavy and white and one thin and black, napkin-ing mustard out of the corners of their mouths, the thin one still holding half a sandwich. They rapped on the windshield and Carl said, "We're in here," as if they couldn't see these two people ash-white and sitting far too still. The heavy cop, badge said Johozowitz, said something to the thin cop, badge said Reilly, and went off to talk to the kid, who began drawing some very complicated picture in the air. Thin cop went to Carl's side and helped him out and asked Rita to wait.

In the wounded and buckled quiet interior of the car Rita watched that kid drop his arms and jump around the sidewalk, watched him play slanted charades with Johozowitz, watched the cop go, Oh, I get it, and put his hand over his badge. The kid began peeling off twenties, pressing the bills into a waiting hand. But Johozowitz is not a name you forget. "Jumping Johozowitz," she said to herself, "Holy Mohozowitz." She said, "Do not move, lovely Rita." She listened to herself and waited. She sang "Lovely Rita, meter maid" in such a thin and plaintive voice that it scared her. She called out her half-broken window, "Is it all right if I get out now?" in that same cracked little whinny.

Kid and Johozowitz were now doing a statement, cop listening carefully with all sorts of due respect.

The thin one came back to Rita's side, said, "Let's try manual extrication." She waited, her head under the ceiling of the Toyota. The officer's dark eyes were watering, his cheeks were mahogany, ruddied from cold. He carefully reached around and punched lightly to push the busted window glass out. As he pulled on the door it gave way with a tremendous, animal-like groan. "Go Reilly," Rita said. He said "I get shit for my name—a black Reilly? they say."

She said, "Black Irish?" He didn't get it. Not a talker. She said, "Anyway. Looks like your friend Johozowitz over there is taking more than a statement."

Reilly said, "Miss, never mind him, we need to think about you." And she tried to formulate a counterpoint, like, *If you don't think about him you're not thinking about me,* but there was another man now, an EMT unbuckling her seat belt, he looked perhaps Filipino or Polynesian, almond eyes, he was cradling her head against some kind of soft plank, his arms were lifting her off her feet, she shut up like an infant as she rose into the air, she let him fold her into a sit on the edge of the curb, let him lean her against the sturdy tire of the white truck, the ambulance, she realized, and blinked in the reddish light strobing around them. And he knelt beside her, unzipped an orange bag and took out various things, a canister, a dial, a clamshell mask. The oxygen tasted like peppermint, she kept inhaling, it was delicious.

"Whoa," he said, and pulled off the mask, "Don't want to get high on that."

"Why not," Rita said, feeling high. "And what happened to my Reilly?"

"Do you think you're really hurt?" the EMT said. "Do you have hot or cold or numb sensations?"

"Are you from Hawaii?" Rita said.

"I'm from dreamworld," he said.

"No, really," Rita started. Shouldn't they be trying to help her be clearer since everything was so unclear?

"She all there?" Reilly said over his shoulder.

"Dreamworld," said the EMT.

"You came back," Rita said, "thanks for asking."

"No, I mean, in your opinion, do you need further treatment? Or do you want to waive your right?" Reilly said.

"What right?"

"To go to the hospital. Or do you want to waive that?"

"We have to go to breakfast," Rita said. "We haven't seen her in so long."

"So, no?" Reilly said.

"I have so much to do," Rita said.

"Do you feel severe pain in your head or neck?"

"Nothing," Rita said.

"Do you know what day this is?"

"Yes," Rita said.

"Do you know what your name is?"

"Yes," Rita said.

"Do you know your name?"

She began to sing the Rita meter maid song. She could not push air out of her mouth to make a strong note. "I'm usually better than this," she explained.

"But you want to say you're okay? So you waive further treatment."

Rita said, "Sure, I'll say that. I'll waive. I love waves, I mean we did at some point drive to the beach, and I stared at the ocean, this huge roll of water up and over the beach, again and again. The red light is like sunset, ever think of that? And my mouth does not want to move clearly, I think."

"I'll do a recheck," said the EMT, timing her pulse, checking her jaw.

As they ministered to her Rita felt herself back away inside. She felt the city quiet down and become softer, felt the morning brightening up to afternoon, and somewhere nearby was Carl, she could hear him talking. And the ambulance washed the stone of the buildings with pink light, and the cars driving by were nice and slow. The young man walked by with blood-shot eyes in a windbreaker, huddling into it. And he gave her a piece of paper and said, "I'm Anthony and there's the number, and you okay? I'm really so sorry," and Rita thought, it's all right, but you only wrote down six numbers. She said, "Yes, I'm absolutely fine." She thought, this is like when you're on the beach, if you just stop moving and calm down enough, you can feel the ocean's power beneath you, the incredible pull and gravity as it wants to pull you back out to sea, and nothing else really feels as important as that.

"He fucked us," Carl said when they got back to their loft.

"I think I'll take a nap," Rita said, and fell into an industrial-strength sleep, thick as cement. Rita would wake up when Carl came over and kissed her on the temple, said "how are you, you waking up yet?" And her temple was sore, his lips pressed too hard, and Rita said, "I think I made a mistake, I wasn't thinking clearly, I think. I think I was distracted, maybe—I can't tie the words down, my mouth is kind of slow."

She told Carl she smelled Chinese dumplings, the pork steam, Carl said no, no dumplings, smiling at her, looking so tired. She said, "He only wrote six numbers," but could not recall who, or what. She was so hungry from that smell. Carl said, "I could order, but why don't we just go right now? Let's go, all right?"

"This doesn't look like any Chinese restaurant I know," Rita said as she entered the MRI tube. Inside God clucked a spring-loaded tongue, whirred along her skull, knocked on the bone and found everybody there.

"I smell incense," Rita said.

They gelled her head and hooked up diodes, Rita sat in a chair and watched the lines scratch over the rolling paper, said, "It's like scoring an orchestra with no hands." When she spoke it made those fickle little arms tremble and spike. "None of that," said the red-haired tester woman, "unless you have to pee. You need to be even-steven."

"Steven wasn't even," Rita said, "he had one ball." She winked at Carl. "Old, old flame."

"Good to know," he said, but kindly.

The tester combed the conductive gel out of Rita's hair, clucked, "There, there, your reading was clear as a bell. Just shampoo double since it's oil-based, did you know that? I didn't. Things you learn when you think you know it all. Just rest, you'll be good as new."

"I haven't been new in thirty years," Rita said.

"There was incense in here recently," Rita said to the doctor, a tall birdlike man with white hair combed over a pink pate. "Can't you smell that? And there was a chrome bird flying out the window. Or a bird whose feathers somehow reflected the sun. And can you tell me why I feel like my voice is slurred?"

"Right," said the doctor, nosing in a file. "Your voice sounds fine to me. And the other things, the—birds, they will go away."

"I like birds," Rita said. "I don't want them to go away. What would the world be like?"

He said, "She is just temporarily confused. She has a common syndrome. The accident or trauma sets off a firing of adrenalin, but the adrenalin keeps firing. It's stuck in on."

"Stuck on," Rita said, rolling a floppy hand lovingly along Carl's pale face. "You," she warbled.

"My girl's got a syndrome?" Carl said.

"Fight or flight," the doctor said. "And the mind will play tricks on itself, go down-down, up-up, then cross the senses— chemically she misfires; physically there is nothing wrong. The senses cross as the brain looks for answers."

"Like crossing legs?" Rita said. "Do I sound like a nut?" She was feeling so giddy. There was a picture of a mountain range on the wall, snowcapped, under an overexposed, impossibly deep blue sunny sky. There was a slogan beneath the photograph: *Climb Every Mountain.*

"That's an awful thing to do to a mountain," Rita said. "So much cliché. It smells like fried eggs."

"You should just go home," the doctor said. "Don't do anything. Try to not even think. Just watch TV. Redundant, non-traumatic focus will usually ease the brain back into shape."

"Brain Fonda," said Rita, and guffawed loudly.

They did not have a television, so first tried a nontelevision method: books and music. Rita said she couldn't concentrate, that reading gave her a headache, all those ants crawling around the page, and music was too emotional and raw, it made her feel so useless, like a rag doll. Then she tried to make a sandwich and put the mustard on the wrong side of the bread and dropped it and collapsed into a heap at the base of the table in the kitchen area and just cried.

"Where's my up-up?" she said. "I need alternatives. And alternative punk rock is a bullshit category and it's over and you know it. I can't listen to another growling vanity case. And I never called Junie back and she must hate me. And those fucking cops who didn't care and their sandwiches, the fucking mustard—"

"I called," Carl said.

"And you talked about sex? You pimping me to her creepo now?"

"I assume this is part of your syndrome," Carl said. He made a habit of shutting the door very softly when he left.

"I did not get to call my friend back about missing breakfast. I am not just some *patient*, and why do you keep leaving me here," she called as the shoe hit the closing door.

Carl came home with a television. "I borrowed it," he said. "No time for the high road, right?"

"Nothing high here," Rita said. The television was enormous. It was the biggest television Rita had ever seen.

"And chocolates," Carl said, thrusting out a fancy box. "So put your fangs away."

"I love you," Rita said, "my butterflies are hearting you. My soul is wrapping you in gilded wings. Somewhere not in industrial Brooklyn I am peak foliage and you are in your Woody station wagon, smoking a pipe and watching me strip. I feel like I want to cry."

"Please don't cry," Carl said, but it was too late.

"Repetitive nontraumatic," he said, setting the television on the dresser right in front of their bed.

Rita sniffed and said, "You are my knight, you are my prince, you are my Carl, you are my Darling Carl. Darlacarl. Darla, how do my dicktate?"

"What?"

Happiness made Rita chatter. She said, "Remember the Buckwheat joke? The teacher says 'Buckwheat, can you use the word dictate for me in a sentence?' And Buckwheat thinks a second and says, 'Oh, I know. Darla, how do my—'"

"Don't be foul," Carl said. "Don't be offensive."

"But I'm allowed to be anything, I have a syndrome," Rita said. "There is nothing to be done. And Doc said television is good for syndromes, it's practically made for syndromes. It will just be me and the syndrome and the television in the loft and we'll be fine. It is the October of my mind and my leaves are falling one by one, and I'll die if I can't touch you. Can't we have sex now?"

Rita had never been one to get involved in other people's lives, was a skeptic to the core at movies. Now she took to the TV like it was her long lost sister, they were one, they were bonded. The television soothed her, talked to her, pulled out feelings that seemed to have nowhere else to go. She could not believe how easy it was to care about Maria the orphan, to laugh at Bart. And the wonderment of children was infectious. If anyone else had been there she might have been embarrassed, but it was just her in the loft. Carl stayed for hours at work across the river, but it wasn't like he stayed away, he just worked hard.

During commercials Rita would get off the bed and go to the window, watch the street below. It was all warehouses, the thunderous rattle of rolling gates, industrial rumble and jounce of trucks over potholes and cobblestones and old trolley tracks, loading and unloading giant barrels, rag bundles, appliances on pallets. Pigeons and tattered plastic bags flew around, coasting on those riverborne gusts, surpassing the low bulk of buildings, snagging on power lines. Down the block the East River turned from slate to blue to green, shimmered in sunlight, whitecapped in wind. Sometimes a lone brown dog jogged down the backbone of the street, so she threw food out the window hoping he'd find it: bread, tunafish, cheese.

"I think I am becoming a sentimental fool," she told Carl one night when he said, "Where's all that cheese we bought?"

There were programs on guessing the number on the wheel, singing the best, the life of presidents, the fastest human, when babies first blink. Commercials for bread, cleanser, lobster restaurants, deodorant. Rita would not let herself stare at the wonderland of the commercials—she'd better have some kind of limit, she decided. She trusted the programs would call her back. And they did: told her when the commercials were over with their little musical hooks.

Around dinnertime she was jogging around the loft, trying to get her blood moving, when she was called back to the television by an old song. It was a lovely song traced by a reedy voice, so peaceful and whimsical, a very green voice, that reminded her of a man at home in a mountainscape. "Rocky mountain high," he sang.

It was John Denver. He was singing "Rocky Mountain High." She had a nostalgic flash from long, long ago, how she would shut her eyes and listen to that song, how the melody felt like denim and rhinestone wings, the word "Colorado" like spring water pouring down from the sun. It always made her want to wear flannel shirts and faded jeans.

A twangy newscaster vaulted over the fading song with a slightly nasal voice, teleprompter syntax, words used as stops: "Went down in water and we do *not* yet know the cause of this *possible* tragedy they are *combing* the waters of Monterey Bay looking for the *American* prince of song while hope is *fading* fast."

"Oh my gosh," Rita said. She sat on the edge of the bed, black-fingernailed hand covering her aghast mouth, eyes welling up.

"Just fifty-three," the newscaster said.

"So young," Rita said.

They showed photos: a big mountain, an old man with blond hair, blond voice, blond guitar, blond face, the wire granny glasses, wearing the old folkie's brown suede vest, fancy watch on his wrist. A photograph of a plane that looked like a white space pod giving the finger, a man's authoritative voiceover: "This is the Long EZ, an experimental aircraft, a thousand pounds of fiberglass—"

"Carl," Rita said on the phone.

"I'm in the middle, you all right?"

"John Denver's plane crashed."

"John *Denver*? Whatever made you think about John Denver?"

"He's on the news. He's only fifty-three. He still looks the same, just more leathery. I'd forgotten all about him. How awful of me. When I was a little girl he sang me to sleep. Aren't you coming home soon?"

"Tonight's that office dinner thing, so no, I can't, I wish—"

The evening darkened into an extra-windy night, and the wind howled around their rickety windows and rattled at the glass. Rita took aspirin, had a little wine, lit a candle on top of the television, said, "Look for the flame, John."

I'm not losing my mind, she told herself. I just have this syndrome, this adrenaline thing. At least she didn't smell things anymore, and her mouth didn't feel so lazy. And in Monterey crowds were holding a vigil by the edge of the bay, candles flickered out into the Pacific. A group of German tourists were standing together, swaying, singing, "Gundry Whoad, Take-a me Whoam—"

"He transcent awl der buntarees," one said in tears.

"Yes," Rita said, welling up, sipping wine. The phone rang, but she might miss something. And there came the divers, rising to the surface, one holding up what looked like a paper plate, cut to reporters.

It was official. He'd flown his plane for about ten minutes.

And then he took a fatal right turn and dove into the Bay.
Eulogies swarmed the teleprompters, droned out by midwest-
erners who'd made it into the big networks, who kept their
hair well trimmed, were so friggin American, but it didn't matter, you couldn't be skeptical all the time, Rita decided. John
Denver was never skeptical, and look at the beautiful songs he
wrote, and I never gave him the credit and now he's gone.

"A peaceful adventurer, lively spirit, a passionate—"

"Say something useful," Rita said back.

"We think he just didn't know the plane well enough. He
just wasn't yet intimate with the plane."

"But he was a born pilot, his father flew, he loved to fly. He
was confident—"

"Ironically he made his fortune with a song called 'Leaving
on a Jet Plane.'"

"Go to hell," Rita told that reporter.

Carl walked in, after midnight, to the entire loft blue and
flickering. Rita was still watching, eyes turned into dehydrated
orbs. "Darling," she said, "You would not believe how much I
love you. Please never learn to fly."

"Flying makes me throw up," Carl said. "But what's that
white gunk all over the top of the television?"

"It was an emotional day," she said.

Rita had to follow the tragedy, as she called it. It's time for
the update on the tragedy. She kissed Carl hastily, her eyes
still watching the talking heads, pointing out the seagulls that
flocked the news crews waiting for a french-fry toss, the air-

craft officials standing somberly in their bureaucratic wind-breakers.

"I'm fine with this," Carl said, "for like another few days, and then maybe we talk to the doctor about something stronger?"

"Sure," Rita said, biting her nails as they flashed stats across the screen about fuel loss. Each day the picture of John Denver's last ten minutes of life became sharper and more awful. "Oh no," she said.

Carl, concerned, came over, half an apple in his hand.

"That smells rancid," Rita said.

"You all right?"

"He didn't gas up the plane," she said. "The ground technician said, 'Don't you think it's a little low?' And John Denver said no. He just wouldn't put more gas in the plane. So the plane ran out of gas, and to switch to the secondary, or the auxiliary, or something additional fuel tank you have to turn around behind you, and reach behind your right shoulder to flick a switch, and when he did that he involuntarily pushed his right foot down, which caused the plane to bank sharply to the right. And he was distracted, so he didn't pay attention. Maybe three seconds he didn't know it was happening. And maybe the afternoon sun bounced into his eyes, because the blue sky was so perfect, and when he looked back out the window he blinked, he couldn't tell for a long moment whether it was the sky or the water, and he blinked again and then realized, *Oh shit, it's the water.*"

"Whoa," Carl said.

"I know."

"No, I mean you."

"Not me," Rita said. "John Denver. He crashed into the Bay nose first. That was it. End of story."

"Take a deep breath," Carl said.

"Can you imagine? Maybe he scared the seals as he hit the water. Maybe he dove right through a pack of salmon, and the plane sank into a bed of kelp waving like smitten fans, *sing more, sing more.*"

Imagining this, retelling it for Carl, had brought something to the surface. Rita began to sob as if the core of the earth had decided to cough itself up through her body. She was coughing at the same time. Carl took hold of her and patted her back, and she grabbed onto his arms and would not let go.

"Can you imagine," she said, "Can you?"

"You're hysterical."

"Can you? Seeing it? The world seeming to rocket up and away from you at a zillion miles an hour? And that's it? That's it?"

"He was probably out," Carl said.

"What if he wasn't?"

"He was knocked out. I'm certain. Blunt force trauma. You said they found the plane in pieces. Something would have hit him and knocked him out. He didn't feel a thing."

"I can't breathe," she said, coughing. "Nothing, nothing makes any sense."

Later, when Rita was calmer, the spasms over, they lay in bed, side by side, like on a life raft, Rita said, in the middle of the ocean. "Talk to me," she said. "I could just fall off, it feels like." So Carl told her how he'd covered "Leaving on a Jet Plane" in his high school thrash band, screamed it as loud fast as he could, and he lost his voice for a week afterwards. And his big brother thought it was blasphemy, was a folkie to the core, had those granny glasses and the shag haircut for a while, which Carl washed in green poster paint once.

"I told him I'd wash his hair," Carl said, "and my brother must've thought, great, my little brother is going to wash my hair? He was that gullible, maybe from listening to John Denver. Not gullible," he retracted, when Rita frowned at him, her loyalty tested now, "but so openhearted, as if everyone would always try their best, be sincere and never hurt each other."

And Rita told Carl how when she was a little girl she saw John Denver sing somewhere. It was a big concert out in a summery field. And she was holding her mother's hand, they were rocking back and forth and it was nighttime, and her mother was rapt, her face shining in the moonlight, and she wore a yellow dress, and a kerchief, and sneakers with no laces, and Rita knelt by the sturdy happiness of her mother's shins and looked up into the black starry sky.

And then, at about fourteen, when she and her mother fought all the time, she'd rejected John Denver and all he stood for. She'd stomped on one of his records with her new motorcycle boots and whipped it with the long chain she attached to her wallet. Then she dyed her hair black and lined her eyes and did a blood pact with her best friend that no sugarcoated

American cheese folkie was going to make them look like soft-ies, and that was like in 1980-something, and now she felt so guilty.

In the morning Rita awoke feeling like she'd been asleep for a week, with a massive headache and a sore throat. The roses she'd asked Carl to buy for John Denver were brown, the stalks softening, and they had leached all their red dye into the water of the vase. The color sickened her, it was like true blood, so she went out to the roof. The sun was coming up, a flock of pigeons landed on a nearby water tower and took off again. She went to the side of the roof and threw the roses and the vase and the water over the edge into the junkyard next door, and watched the amazing grace of the flowers plummeting four stories.

Back inside, two newscasters were commentating again. The salt-and-pepper-haired man opined that John Denver was one of those rare artists who preferred joy to sadness, some-thing perhaps from John Denver's early training in est. The frosted blond nodded at his wisdom. A camera cut to a pan of Monterey Bay, the sun glinting down on its innocent water. There was a dais set up on the shore, white bunting whipped in the wind. And a small woman in a cowboy hat solemnly climbed the steps to the little platform, wearing a tidy little flannel shirt tucked into tiny little jeans, fancy embossed cow-boy boots, and something on her shoulders.

"Mrs. Denver is wearing one of her husband's shirts," the newscaster said in a low, we're-at-the-golf-course voice.

"She's wearing one of her husband's shirts," the other one twanged. "We sure hope it gives her comfort."

The woman walked up to her place at the microphones. She had the piercing blue eyes, the crow's feet and high cheekbones of a southwestern-bred beauty in middle age, but looked well kept, groomed, diamond and gold earrings caught the light under the brim of her hat. She was clearly the wealthy California celebrity wife suddenly thrown into the dark cloud of widowhood, and she started her address in a shaking little voice: "Perhaps John was our Icarus, but that was his only mistake. And people made fun of him for wanting to go to the moon, but he was a nature boy with the soul of an astronaut. He was the sunshine on my shoulders, the road to take me home." Her voice cracked, and she said, in a tiny little dietetic voice, "And now, god willing, you are finally home."

"Yes," Rita said. The newscasters were shuffling their papers, getting ready to ruin it. She turned off the television. The loft was so quiet. She could hear Carl, still sleeping, breathing in, breathing out. She walked over to the wall, where her old acoustic guitar hung by its neck on a big yellow hook. She got it down and began to strum and sing, more like intone, clearing her throat and then not even trying to push it:

> *Single engine plane, like a nervous bird*
> *coughed and fell into the ocean, nose first*
> *and now he's gone, little blond man*
> *now he's gone.*

"You're sort of singing," said Carl sleepily.

"It sucks," Rita said, ear bent to tune the strings. "But I felt like it."

Carl, barefoot, came over and sat down. He looked at her. He looked like he was mulling something over, so Rita said, "Yup, feeling all right." She felt kind of emptied out, dehydrated. She said, "It would be nice to be made out of spring water and fresh air."

"Instead of?"

"Grit and muscle parts."

"Muscle parts," Carl said, watching Rita slice a lemon and squeeze it into her tea. Last time he'd watched her in the kitchen, she'd dropped the mustard knife, dropped the bread, dropped down to the floor. "But muscle's strong," he said.

"Overtaxed poisoned muscle parts," she said. "Starved on a diet of concrete and smoke. I'm not saying there's anything wrong with beating your head against the wall, but when someone comes out of nowhere and just stops you dead—"

"You're not dead," Carl said. "We have absolutely established that."

"Just the idea," Rita said. "But more than that? When I close my eyes? I see blue."

"What?"

"Squeeze your eyes shut," she said to Carl. "What do you see?"

"Orange," he said, keeping them shut. "A need for caffeine." He got up to make his coffee.

"I see blue," she said. "It may just be cathode-ray blue, not mountain blue. But his wife, she's in the same place. She is listening to the advice of lawyers, and signing things, but she's looking at the horizon and blowing kisses to her flier all the time."

"I'm not sure what you're saying," Carl said.

"Just that we race around, we grind ourselves down."

"You going to go watch more TV?" Carl said.

"I turned it off," Rita said. "I'm done."

She took her tea and went to the dresser, and began rummaging through drawers. Her body had lost some of its padding lately, Carl noticed as she leaned over. He could see the ridges of her vertebra as her shirt crept up, a sweet landscape exposed.

Carl said, "That kid who hit us? That cop he paid to look the other way?"

"Anthony, Johozowitz," Rita said.

"They want us to give some kind of report. You up to it? Can you remember?"

"I remember everything," Rita said. "I just didn't think about it. But it's right there."

Carl came home after lunch on the day they were supposed to go give their report. He looked nervous. He had worn a jacket, something he never did. "Should I wear a tie?" he called to Rita, who was getting dressed in the bathroom. "I really don't even want to do this. What could possibly help about it?"

Rita came out. "Howdee," she said. She was wearing a flannel shirt and jeans, old cowboy boots. Gone were her mascara, her purple lips.

"You've lost it," he said. "I am already so exhausted. Should we skip it?"

"We should do it. We have to. Fight or flight."

There was a lawyer sitting in the deposition room. He had a well-trimmed mustache, and his name was Gold. "No way," Rita said, delighted, poking Carl in the ribs. Carl loosened his tie. "Good idea," Gold said. "We have about 125 questions."

"Who do you represent?" Carl said.

"The other guy," said Gold.

They waited for Carl and Rita's lawyer, McShea, who hustled in with a thick briefcase and started slapping forms on the table. He was a small, quiet looking man, a shock of red thistle on his head, and he arched an orange eyebrow at Rita's outfit but said nothing. He shook Carl's hand. Rita said, "So you know each other?"

"Carl did the legwork," McShea said.

"Ah," Rita said.

"While you were working on things," Carl said to Rita with a meaningful expression.

The men shuffled papers. Rita volunteered to test the microphone and the tape recorder. She used an old stage joke: "Skeleton walks into a bar, orders a beer and a mop—"

No one got it.

"Testes, testes," she said giddily, and clapped when it replayed.

Gold used words like *supposed* a lot, *purported*, *speculative*, *debatable*, until what rang loudest was the fluorescent fixture buzzing above their heads. "Supposedly contracted a temporary and not unusual syndrome," he said, "with reputed slight psychological effects with a duration of two weeks at most."

At that Carl lost his cool and slapped the table, to which Gold smiled and said, "I'm not done. You'll have your chance."

When it got to the deposing part, Gold's questions were not so much asked as lobbed, mostly at Rita, since she had seen the purported exchange. Purported this, purported that, he seemed to be saying. No, Rita would say. I *saw*.

After a dozen questions she felt like a carcass, and saw Carl with his head buried in his folded arms on the table, and she felt something disengage, heard the buzzing above her, and suddenly the lines got crossed again. "Is it that easy?" she asked out loud. "Do you have any idea what is happening?" she asked Gold. "Do you? The rampant, rancid abuses of power?"

"Excuse me?" he said irritably. "Will you please just describe the scene one more time?"

She said, "The sky was white, and there was this pigeon. And we were going to see Junie, despite what her slimebag boyfriend wants. And boom. Then Johozowitz was covering his eyes with his hand."

"Eyes?" Gold pushed.

"Hand," Rita corrected.

"Maybe we're not ready for this," Carl said to McShea, who cupped the microphone.

"It's a little late," McShea said.

Gold turned to Rita. "Do you remember how you felt?"

"Bleak," Rita said. "I was a lead singer before all this, just like she was a millionaire's wife, but somehow there's an up-front element in both of our lives. And now there's this dark parallel. The ability of machines to plummet, to maim."

"And the street?" Gold was unmoved by any of this poetry.

"Gold Street," Rita said. "Named after the lawyer."

Still no sign he was actually listening.

"And the light was green?"

"Green as the prairie in springtime," she said.

He looked up. "Are you certain?"

"We were talking about things, and I saw that it was green, so we'd have time to buy cigars. I am sure. And the car was blue. A bad, metallic, cheap American blue. Red pinstripes. Like a flag."

Gold turned to McShea. "I'm not sure what you think this will accomplish," he said.

"Accomplish my ass," Rita said. "Johozowitz took the money. I saw. Should I sing about it? Should I tell the newspaper?"

"That's it," said Gold. "We are over."

Outside, McShea lit a cigarette. "Should I tell you what I think?" he said.

Rita said, "Did that room smell like sweat? Just tell me it did."

"It really did," Carl said.

"That was probably me," said McShea.

The holidays were coming, snow coming down like dirty ash. They had breakfast with Junie, who told them she'd caught her boyfriend with her sister and that was that. The junkyard next door took their Toyota. They worked on some songs, the same edgy ditties they'd done before. But their hearts weren't in it. Carl said he just felt wiped out. Rita strummed her old acoustic, watching pigeons and birds. Soon as she got home from her temp job she'd skim off her cheap suit and get into her flannel shirt.

They thought they'd never hear anything else about the accident, that the cruel wheels that turn the city had just picked up the mess in their treads and rolled it away. But one February day, as freezing rain pinged down and coated the old cobblestones with a sheen of treacherous ice, an express-mail truck skidded to a stop in front of their building. Its rushed driver rang their buzzer relentlessly, and Rita found a damp envelope in her hands. It was a check. It was a lot of money, more than they might ever see at one time again in their lives. It seemed to come from a charitable organization. They couldn't tell. Something called PBAVC234#2, LLC.

"LLC," Carl said. "Limited liability." They told McShea.

"Don't tell me," he said. "And you never heard me say anything crazy, like just throw it in the bank, shut up and have a good life."

"You really think," Rita said. "Really?"

"Did you not hear me say what I did not say? Now go have a life," said McShea.

They pinned a photograph of John Denver to the ceiling of the new car, right above the passenger seat, so you didn't actually see it, but it was like a halo over your head. The picture was from when he was young and un-veneered, face turned upwards to the sky, mouth open in song, one wiry arm around the waist of his guitar. The car wasn't actually new, it was an old Plymouth from an obsessive restorer in Coney Island. It was wrapped in so much metal that Anthony and his car would have accordioned into a cartoon if he hit them. It was a good car for driving, a good car for heading west. Its trunk could hold a small herd of suitcases and four guitars. Its hood cleaved the open highways with a big boat's certainty, and when you turned the wheel it seemed to already have switched direction.

They pulled back onto the highway after a Waffle House stop, Carl humming as he palmed the wheel. Rita traced the long lines on the road atlas, hundreds of miles away from the tangle of the northeast.

"Colorado?" Carl said.

"Carlarado," Rita said.

They drove a while. Carl eased around a convoy of semis, in a groove.

"This car has steering so powerful," Rita said, "that you can breathe to the left and it veers like a plane." Then she stopped and said, "No. It doesn't do that at all."

She set the atlas on the dashboard, and leaned her legs out the window to catch the Western sun.

GALLETAS

for S.P.

That March was a month of storms, the aloe plants in a constant state of alert, quivering warnings with their nervous points. The monsoons came like tiptoe hands over the mountains, then vaulted into bruising, thunderous things. And one afternoon we were sitting on my porch eating those pale crackers we always ate, the galletas: little medallions of flour and salt and lard. We were savoring them, chewing slowly, it would be our last time. We were three girls, the red-haired girls, our red hair shone triple insults into the tannic air. The tube of crackers had a label with a florid name and a florid picture: it said *Galletas Victoria* in romantic script, over a portrait of a black-haired Indian maiden. Her blue eyes flashed fire at any intruders, she was saving Mexico from the white man a hundred years ago and every day since. Sentimentally I pocketed the label, made a pact to never throw her away.

The wind picked up and our red hair did backflips, flashed

copper to the coming storm. And Lucy sitting on the old armchair in her oopsydaisy little calico dress said to pale, pale Margerita, *You look so luminous, you look like a glowworm.* And Margerita toed some dust with her shuffleboot and did an aw-shucks. The light was metallic. Ozone rolled its chocolate malt smell over us and clouds whitecapped against the too-fast front above and the hills darkened and fifty miles away, at the airport, my plane found its tricky white line through the gusts and taxied up to the snaking terminal to drop off seventy-five people and then refuel and re-snack and in about two hours, reload.

I would be there. I was leaving. I was giving up the desert and the West and heading back to the land of nor'easters and heavy coats. For no good reason but a broken heart, that perpetual ticket to ride. Months and months I had been staring down the street towards that boy's house like there was the horizon, if I could just get inside his door we could dive right back into that perfect ocean, float on his mattress on the floor. And Lucy was with that yellow-haired kink, the ex-army guy who still wore green and had that wet stare. And Margerita was getting over that gap-toothed kid, the one who could tripletap a whole other solo during feedback. And we ate galletas and drank one last beer and piled my bags on the sidewalk by the prickly pear.

Everything I could take on a plane except the dog was in those bags, everything else bequeathed to a bonfire, which they promised to have in the desert on my behalf. I had that dog then, that half-wild thing who had a nose like a geiger counter,

found treasure in dust all the time. She paced the yard's invisible lines, uprooting old bones, nosing the acrid webs the black
spiders wove against the house. It was a ramshackle house, a
frayed-wire firebox, an insect and mouse house, but it would
be a year before a toaster sparked its kindling and took out half
the street. And Margerita threw the dog a biscuit, a moon sailing off the porch into a toothy mouth. Margerita far from her
breakdown, the tranking, blurry-headed shock, and Lucy with
no babies yet, and my dog still alive. My dog lifted her bitch leg
against the fence along the front yard, the fence that refused to
stand up or fall down, and the dry, dry grass around her rasped
in the coming winds, whispered longingly against her flanks,
let the dust swirl up into a banshee as flint struck off the dis-
tant peaks, and I said I had to go.

My dog commenced her sniff of the big yard she'd never
see again. A dog remembers, a dog forgives and forgets, is what
I clung to. Five years in the desert I watched her answer all
her own questions, a marvel, really: where the biscuit crumb
was, where the spiderwebs, where that long-ago dead bird.
Her nose was the careful avoider, recording placements and
positions over and over: the biscuit crumbs, the spiders, the
bones, the people, where the cats rubbed their vain musk and
people laughed in notes like skipstones and loved her long ears
with their hands. And her ears swiveled in the direction of the
van door opening, telling us it was therefore time to go past
the mountains and run through the old dry wash to the south.
And her tail wagged, agreeing ahead of time to be taken to
the old dry wash, the long-ago riverbed that still gives off the

scent of fresh water after the rain, that gives up its bones so easily. Foolery, to agree to anything ahead of time, I thought, too easy for someone to trick you, and then I did, slipping a travel pill hidden in biscuit down my dog's distracted, trusting throat.

My fellow red-haired girls handled the bags like they were minor insults. Hefted my life into the van. Hefted the dog's airline crate into the van. Hefted me into the van and the dog into the van. The storm caught up and shrieked like Jezebel and pushed the van all the way down the highway, the sideways rain racing across the windows in words. Lightning turned the sky chartreuse, razzed the tarmac of the short-term lot. Testy wind stole the dollar away from the dollartaker's slow hand. And then we stood together in the gale, us three, our red hair igniting. My dog mumbled from the travel pill and stood woozy and splayed in the dying-down rain. My throat closed up and opened and closed and opened. Red-haired girls often say hello and do not say very good goodbyes. Red-haired girls keep their hearts quietly inside. The storm went back to the mountains to take a nap and let the sun bounce around the valley. My red-haired girls dragged the bags across the tarmac as far as the open-close doors to the terminal and would go no farther, nowhere nearer the canned happyland inside. They were girls in the wind. And behind me and the dog the doors gave a clear glass retort and I turned to watch those two red-haired girls do their shuffleboot sass back to the van, the now theirs van, and pull away with the speed of the falling.

WHY I GOT FIRED

Being nineteen and fearless. About to lap-dance the trickster who'd unzipped in the dark. Jumping off the rude guy and then clocking him in the jaw. Shoving stale popcorn in his face as he grabbed. Bouncer Tom come to my rescue, come to lift him out, chair and all before he could zip it in. All the men laughing as the fool hung out of his trousers. All the girls cheering as he tumbled out the doors. *Free beers on the house and no one try that again with my girls. But you,* said the owner all dressed in black with a comb-over, *I know you're 36-26-36 but you make too much trouble. Go cool your troublemaker heels at my other place down the road.*

Dancing at the joint down the road where the DJ nicknamed me Brick House. Bribing the DJ to play "Brick House." The spotlight shimmering off the red sequined strip. Owning the room while sporting that red sequined strip. The flannel and boot crowd fumbling pocket change under the strip, rough fingers and no finesse. Loving the moves and hating the men, loving the men and hating the moves, hating the moves for making me hate the men, who love the moves and probably hate me, but jump back into their cold Cleveland cars to love themselves handily before returning home.

And trying to keep it simple trying to keep it simple trying to keep it simple and *If you can't*, said the DJ, *try one of these little blue buddies instead.*

That place was called Brown's. That rough bar gone rougher come the deep freeze of winter. Come the deep freeze of winter in northern Ohio. The stink of fry-pit perch from the bar buffet, fry-pit smokestack greasing the icy sky. Boy shot sandbags open with his BB gun, poured sand to help cars grip the endless ice. Sundown by mid-afternoon throwing night down too early.

One Friday night when the heat pipes froze I wouldn't take it all off. Glass of beer flying at my crotch from a table of bad bored. Cold beer white skin goosebumps hopping down malt-stained thighs. Next night dancing naked with the fever caught from dancing wet the night before. Next day home under blankets in the ramshackle on Morgan Lane, red sequins still glued on and glinting under the covers like embers in a died-down fire.

Cleveland rock 'n' roll Cleveland. Fifteen-mile shiver in a gasket-blasted Pacer. Fifteen miles down the balky break-down-anytime road between Brown's and the ramshackle on Morgan Lane. Fifteen shiver miles singing the chorus to "Brick House" to stay warm. Night road the dark outstretched arm of a big sorry man. Pointing thataway girlie, seven more miles to go and it's Hello Cleveland All-Nude and All-U-Can-Eat same place same time same price.

Me on a bender. Hump-dancing a man's wife onstage, me on the bender, she on a dare. Making more money pretending to fuck her than any other night. That night's tips bought another month in the ramshackle on Morgan Lane. Wondered if I should give her some money as she turned away from the cheers suddenly pale and sick with shame.

Me in a rut. Me in a rut on another sub-zero night-time afternoon. Seven sad men in the bar and me trying to dance to Bob Seger, the spiteful sad barmaid's insisted-on favorite. Bob Seger the worst unfunky. Can't do any moves but white-girl herky jerky. Seven men watching from scattered seats around the room. Seeing the bearded landlord of that ramshackle on Morgan Lane in the scattered shadowy seats of the seven men watching. My landlord sitting there watching like a sin professor, chewing the fat cud of what-a-surprise.

Landlord come to my side door next morning and scratched his flaky beard onto the side door steps and gave me the up-and-down with wet-lips and eyes. I smack the side door spring-shut right in his face. His phone call ten minutes later, his deep breaths between the words *I'll need an increase or else if you know what I mean is that anyway to treat your landlord* as the morning toast burnt in the fiery-wire toaster. Deep breath and hell-bent nerves firing and telling him that if he tried to kick me out I'd tell his wife everything and I wouldn't mince words and who do you think she'll believe? Taste of burnt toast conjuring up the sound of a landlord breathing. Taste of burnt toast forever ruined by the landlord who made himself a regular at Brown's and outstayed me there by his whole life.

New city five years later. Twenty-four and hungry in the new city under the sunbelt sun. Twenty-four and hungry in a city of toupee-white-belt-powder-blue-leisure suits. All bad tippers getting their Sanka from career waitresses who'll never leave their jobs. Job cross-off after job cross-off. Walking jobless down the road to the big magenta sign. White girl in a top hat hip-cocked and grinning on the big magenta sign.

Falling back on a skill because it pays easy money. Forgetting it's not easy, sometimes not even money. Losing the tips in my T-strap to a swift-fingered frat boy in the new city. A big roach crawling in my wig in the dressing room of the new bar. Tables of thin beer and boat shoes and cheap tropical shirts. Shorts so thin you could get a disease doing a lap-dance.

And one day a lady in a headband, a prim lady with hair the color of corn, swept back from her powdered brow in a velvet headband. Prim headband lady walks in with a shaft of rude sun and says she wants to dance. Wants to audition and dance for the men. Wants to meet all the girls and see what it's all about. *Show me how to dance for the men show me how to do it what else do you do?* All questions no legwork no waist no chest no good. *They say you can't take it all off but don't you take it all off?* Prying like a little sister only asking to get you in trouble, surprise over dinner when she tells your parents what you said.

Don't tell me you can't make more money after you dance, don't you make the real money that way? I won't tell, don't you think I could do it too? Girls pawing the floor in their fishnets like a wary herd. Girls looking for exits. *What girl you know comes to strip in a headband* said the old blondie wiping oil into her chest as the lady took her headband back out the door and down the road.

Hours crawling towards night. Rank sunset coughing up a sallow moon. Glasses clanking onto shelves barmaid setting up cigarettes stubbed down. Moths swarming in the headlights as cars pull up too close, high beams swimming the floor through the windows. Car doors chuffing shut too loud, too same-time, too many car doors shutting too loud and all at the same time.

Headlights flashlights front door badge glints men shout. Waiting a split second too long. Waiting a split second too long before the bolt. Whole herd of girls in flimsy this and that trying to beat it to the bathroom to the window out the back. Headband lady giving the megaphone a blowjob. Big lady officer in grey and blue with a piece. The Mama Sarge of the whole shebang. Girls with stories, girls with memories tucked under their supposedly impervious animal-thick skin, with gut radar, antennae firing and legs jolted to move. Mascara panic running. Heels clomping, shoes flicked off to stocking feet. Making it halfway down the back hallway which was making it absolutely nowhere at all.

Line of sass girls led out into the headlight glare. Line of sass girls fuming in flexi-cuffs, handcuffed by the new city's PD. Flap of more vice-badge wallets like show-off card tricks. Hand on my head pressing me into a back seat, cop climbing in too, squad car door chuffing shut. What's the difference be-tween vice and vise. Choke meat smell of burgers just eaten in the back seat. Chortle and click of radio set on low. Wrappers and cuffs and tangle of more flexis in the back seat. Vinyl gain-ing grip on the bare skin of my back leg.

Officer Somebody Big Man making cowboy talk in the back seat. Making quick clumsy fondle. Making dig for the goods. Mustache crumbed with lunch, flexi-cuffs keeping blood from hands, vinyl bite at skin shift. Scratch of trouser leg and bigfoot black shoe and *Say my name.* Biting lips to not do, not say. Thigh muscle lockdown. Grim stare. Count to ten knees locked shut. Dancing means muscles. Dancing muscles saved the dancing girl.

Twenty-four and hungry in the stationhouse chair in the empty belly of the profitless night. Twenty-four staring at powdered donuts on the stationhouse donut table. Cup of sour coffee, quiet stretch of soremuscle legs. Blondie walk-ing in behind the Mama Sarge walking out behind the Mama Sarge. Blondie's chest still shining with oil, a grit-tooth swal-low running down her old throat, her beach-witch hair falling dankly down. Fingers pressed to inkpad, fingers bumped to paper. Officer Somebody like it's post-roundup on the chapar-ral talking post-game with Mama Sarge. Being booked by the new city's PD for soliciting Officer Somebody. *She insisted, I swear. She wanted me.*

The seersucker-suited whiskey-breath sour-gut lawyer come in after his breakfast summoned by a phone call. Grabbed a jelly donut and said *Here's the drill.* Seersucker-suited whiskey-breath sour-gut lawyer with sugar on his grizzle who got me off and then got off. I signing for my effects in the stationhouse, ziplock bag and wanting to fake my name. Sunblast outside the terrible shine of the squad cars lined up in their stalls.

Shrug and change and shower and get back to work. Shrug and work and shower and change and work. Going back to work and just dancing, stretching sore legs against the pole. Thirst come on like a virus. Needing a water pitcher onstage or I panic. Endlessly parched and desert-stranded thirsty and not knowing why. Gulping water after water and careless about anything giving hands a wide berth. Stray dollars grabbed instead of let under elastic, a barren stretch of girlskin and few tips and I didn't care. Water pitchers filled and emptied, gulping from the spout. A night and another night and still thirsty and then a drunk calling me a whore.

You gonna shake it for your Daddy or what

Stopping mid-dip just staring under lights. Arms fall down from the wings of a shimmy. Looking for the face, red screwed up drunk face, long face hollowed out luckless and raw.

Can't stand these uppity attitude types stand there like we wanna watch them think

Stopped mid-dip just staring out at the voice in the room. Stopped and let myself think. Amazed under lights. Thinking, there it is. What I've been missing. My launchpad, my gatecard, my carkey, my doorbell. A reason to fight. Disco ball a siren swirl before my eyes. Drunk standing up back, puffed out chest, a blessed idiot messenger come all this way from nowhere, just for me, all riled up now just for me.

Why you stop dancing you stupid girl get the lead out

Just him, just me. Him the bum-rushed downluck fool in the chair and me the not-so-young meat onstage. Him the doubledare do your job know your place and me the sudden thinker. Thinking, I know why I've been thirsty. All the pieces falling into place like sequins on the red strip. This is the green light, his face, I've got the motor gunning no brakes down that black arm of the road. I'm a grip on the pitcher handle, heft it up the big cool belly of the water pitcher newly refilled. Draw back shoulder like a bow and arrow. There's an Amazon in me. Recoil, ready with a big arc, a cascade of water, a perfect sprung arc off the stage and right into that red standing face, a full pitcher of water in perfect delivery landing smack-dab on the man's mean face.

Glorious wave and splash and filigree of beading on eyelashes and open red mouth. Glorious record skip as the bar cuts the music and the girls come to watch. Glorious perfect legs moving springing off the stage, glorious manager heading consternatedly my way as the glorious agendas of all the losers in the world collide in the ruined interchange, a jumble of cars about to crash. Glorious hands out and ready waiting for a man's naked silly neck and yelling *This one's for Cleveland.*

THE FATHER

One afternoon when he's already done with work and I'm home after school, my father digs a picture out of the shoebox and hands it to me. It's a black-and-white snapshot, wallet-size, of him at twenty-one and beaming in a khaki uniform, standing at ease alone in front of a long wall—the side of a barracks or a mess hall. His hands are buried in the pockets of his pressed trousers, his shoulders are thrown back a little, there's an easy tilt to his hips. In his smile the teeth are very white and his hair is cut into a neat brush, meeting at his brow in a widow's peak.

I was a sergeant then, he says. He's told me things before: he rose quickly and had a platoon, a group of nice guys who cleaned the mess floor so well they got a medal, which my father still has—from the days, he says, when war was fun. He thought up their winning plan—just clean as if you're trying to clear away any trace of yourself; mop yourself into the corner and then slip out the door. The room will be spotless.

I say, Dad, it's a great picture, you look so happy. He's smiling now, too, but it's a different look and his hairline has receded beyond his widow's peak. He takes back the picture and goes into his study, where the radio has big band music on, Bronx boy DJ on a community college station, playing the old favorites. Sometimes I think, Doesn't my father care that the boy didn't grow up on those songs? But to my father it's as if he did—he forgets details like that, generation stuff.

That night we have a cookout, steak for dinner. Dad turns it at the grill while whistling "In the Mood." It's a good cut of steak, sizzling, a large piece he's looking forward to. We set the backyard table with Chinette and plastic forks, Mom's choice, pure white. The sky was fine before but now it's threatening so we're a little wary. But it looks like it'll hold, my mother says. Dad keeps turning the big steak.

There's a rumble, a low rumble and a louder one, then another, the sky's getting darker in that sudden, change-of-weather way. Daddy's hands dive into his pockets. I can't see his face, but I do see that his yellow shirt is damp with sweat and his waist looks thick, extra with age. Another rumble—the sky's turning periwinkle, gray, purple—and I realize he hasn't moved, he's looking down, toward the steak. In the snapshot he and his platoon had just won the medal for cleaning floors and, he said, That was a fine sendoff. The next day we were shipped to Osaka to clean up there, in 'forty-five.

The yard is filling with wind now, the grass I'm staring at is blurring and shiny with new rain. I look up again and Dad is gone. In his place is the air vibrating, and the grill tongs heading for the ground, hitting nose first.

RUSSIAN LOVER

December 12, 1989

Dear Mrs. Watson,

I'm writing to you because here it is, a year later, and it is nearing another Christmas, and I still so acutely regret the fact that the last time we saw each other I made such a mess. I am very sorry that I broke your serving dish and that china platter and the other items. And broke the mirror and ruined the goose. And destroyed the rug, if I did. Did I? I'm not entirely sure what to call what I did. But I do feel this very strong need to apologize to you directly, but in writing.

How are you and Mr. Watson? He still humming? How does he do that? He must have tremendous sinus cavities to generate that much volume. Sorry, but I have always marveled at that and now that we're not going to be in-law relations anymore, for some reason, I find myself kind of nostalgic for you and Mr. Watson. And are you still keeping that dog in the kitchen, that golden retriever that couldn't sit or lie or stand still?

As for me, I am all right. I still work part-time at the same cookbook publisher in midtown. And other than that I am mostly working on writing this letter before the year is over. It is part of my plan to make amends, comb out the snarls of the recent past and start a new life.

Not that I consider Josiah a snarl. Quite honestly, Mrs. Watson, I hadn't really planned on starting a new life this soon. I mean—to be 26 and already heading into a divorce? But anyway, if you were around here on this dark and rainy December night—I mean in the Little Italy/Chinatown area, where sometimes you can smell almond cookies on one corner and garlic frying in olive oil on the other—and if you stood on this block of Mott Street right off Grand, you could look into the windows of this coffee shop. You would see a dark-haired girl sitting in a window booth by herself, bowed over the table as she writes in her notebook (where I am drafting this letter), picking at a plate of french fries and sipping at a cup of coffee, and that would be me, Amy Impellizeri Watson, soon to be just plain Impellizeri again.

Enclosed is $40 to reimburse you for any expenses involved in cleaning up the dining room last Christmas.

I am sending this money because I'm sure you didn't hire anyone to help you clean up, being so Yankee and frugal. I thought Josiah might help clean it up. I thought that was why he wasn't leaping out of his chair to (1) stop me from throwing the goose and the gravy and the peas and the wineglass, and then (2) stop me from running out of the house and far far away.

But instead of trying to catch me before I fell out of grace entirely, he just sat there. Not atypical for him, actually. I remember that night: I turned back before I ran out of the house totally sobbing, close to if not in hysterics. Because I had just found out before we sat down for dinner that *he had been sleeping with this Russian woman.*

You see, Mrs. Watson, that's what happened. Right before dinner the husband I had not seen for 3 months told me he'd been sleeping with another woman.

Anyway I remember that when I turned back before I ran out of the house totally crying, he was just sitting there, still at the table. In fact you were all sitting there, in those highback chairs. And meanwhile I'd cracked that room wide open—gravy slithered down your 18th-century Chippendale mirror, the goose splayed across the rug, expelling its grease into the heirloom pile, shards of china and glass everywhere, that thick expensive wine bloodying the walls, the creamed peas and onions scattered down the hallway floor like the beach at low tide.

And no one made a move. All that food continued to soak into the room and the hallway. And no one made a move to help me either. Not Mr. Watson, not Josiah, not your other son, the lunkish Thaddeus, or his pregnant wife Maria, pronounced with an "eye"—I mean where do you all find each other?—not angelic Penelope or her environmentalist husband, not even Lila (who I thought was my friend) or her fiancé, who I thought kind of liked me because he's from New Jersey too and we're both stocky and dark instead of willowy and light. And certainly not Thaddeus and Maria's little son Washington, who sat there looking sterner than anyone in that absurd little bow tie.

I mean, I stood there for a second, at the threshold of the dining room. And I was such an ugly wreck. And Mozart was tootling on in the background. And I said to Josiah in front of everyone, "Oh my god, I can't believe you're leaving me," and then looked at all of you so you could understand what had just happened and *maybe*—and I know I was just in such a state right then, so it was a feeble attempt to be strategic—you'd suddenly realize that perfect Josiah had done something terrible to me and say *something*. Especially you, Mrs. Watson. I think I said, What should I do?

You met my appeal with an icy gaze and your hands remained folded primly at the edge of your plate, as all around your family lipids and acids ate into the furniture, soaked into plaster. Viscous stuff slithered between glass and frame and I felt like that was the substance between us. Contained, it looks very attractive. But I had exposed the facade.

I should probably make this $80 instead. I know that rug was from Great Aunt Penelope, that she probably got it from her Great Aunt, who got it from some ancestor who had procured it from some nomadic novelty peoples back in the 18th century, probably for a cracked horn of gunpowder or a broken pewter spoon. You are all so grounded in your treasures within that house of yours, the ancestral roots tangling all through the rooms. Maybe by breaking some of that stuff and stirring things up, I did you all a favor. Then you guys could actually not be so repressed and actually talk about your feelings. Because honestly, Mrs. Watson, and I only say this as an outsider now—and no one is more of an outsider than the ex-spouse who is completely out of favor and who the favorite son has decided to divorce, as if to punish her for his bad behavior—now *that* takes self-esteem. If Josiah had been a bit more in touch with his feelings in the first place, would he have gone and done what he did? Have a torrid affair with some cabbage eater the entire fall and not say a word?

Anyway after I had slammed the door to really punctuate my exit, I sat on your front porch under the spruce boughs and Christmas wreaths, sobbing and shaking like a sudden orphan. That hale New England street was totally empty, all those houses enclosing more families like yours. Maybe a cat ran by. The shadows across the snow were very creepy. And *no one* came to get me. So I can only assume that you all sat there, expressing some form of blue-blooded surprise. And then someone, probably Penelope, namesake of that long line of aunts, began to clear the plates. And the men sat there being silent in masculine ways while the women dutifully undid my little tantrum. And no one said a thing—certainly not like, I hope she's all right.

In a way I wish it had ended there. I meant to gather up my strength and run away. But it was really cold. I was wearing a minidress. I know it wasn't exactly dramatic to stand on the porch banging on the front door and demanding to be let in-side again. And that's why, when someone finally opened the door, I ran inside and right up the stairs and locked myself in the attic. My intention was to hurl Josiah's things around the room and try to find a picture of *her*, his Russian lover, some-where. I was sure he had one. Or evidence, something more tangible, with more details, than what he had so vaguely said right before dinner.

I need to tell you something.

Mid-fold of tartan scarf, as I put our things away in the at-tic bedroom, the big old bed made up just for our reunion, I hear those words. You were downstairs bustling the Christmas dinner onto the table, Mr. Watson humming along with *Die Zauberflöte*, people laughing festively.

We hadn't seen each other in 3 months and were just about to sit down at a laden table in front of everyone and he said— *I slept with someone.*

I wasn't sure what I had just heard. I noticed, just then, the silver circles floating across the chocolate wallpaper, the cross-eyed look of the old pine dresser, the harum-scarum stacking of old records and books in the corners under the eaves. And hon-estly—like when you're in a car wreck and you don't remember the first moment of impact?—I'm not sure what I said.

He said, In Helsinki.

Helsinki. What I do remember is that saying that word did not mean I had any idea what it meant.

I slept with a woman in Helsinki, he said.

And then I did this strange disconnect, like when the antenna breaks and the radio station goes static. And then I was trying to find the signal again.

I said, Did you say slept with, as in singular? Once? As in one night while you were in Helsinki?

I slept with someone in Helsinki, he said again.

A singular action? Most of my brain was just focusing on the words. Downstairs I could hear the dog howling along with Mr. Watson's humming, little Washington making fire-engine noises. You were calling, *Five minutes*. I did this quick association: five minutes of marriage left.

Josiah had stopped pacing and was now sitting on the edge of an old wing chair we used to like to do it in. How ludicrous, I thought. To be here talking about this, in this room of all rooms, in this house of all houses, this holiday—

Singular past? I said. Just once?

And I realized I was doing calculations, trying to create a mathematical equation that would add up his transgression and get forgiveness, that I was working along some shred of hope that this might actually add up, after a lot of work, to a bunch of nothing.

He thought. He looked miserable.

Singular past?

Not really, he said.

Over? I said.

Not now, he said.

Not now meaning don't *ask* now, or not over now?

He got up and headed downstairs, leaving me choking under the beams. And I wanted to know what I deserved to know, and I deserved to know what I wanted to know, and I wanted to know all sorts of things. Because for a future professor of history that was outrageously vague, don't you think? And it began to eat at me, and then I was really raging, and then I had to go to dinner, and *pretend*, and I couldn't, et cetera, and I think it was when you reached out with your slender cardigan-sweatered arms and tilted your head in that very hostessy way and said, Could you please pass the peas, Amy? that I just let it all explode out of me.

Sorry.

After I had destroyed the dinner and ran outside and demanded to be let back in and ran back upstairs, I was just planning, honestly, to look through Josiah's things to get the details I needed. So here's another $40 to cover the cost of fixing the attic door after the firemen broke it down to get me out.

I guess if I'd heard someone hysterical behind the door and I was a fireman and I couldn't tell what was wrong with her, and whether she was choking or having a heart attack (yes, even girls can have heart attacks, as they told me in the truck when they gave me oxygen and calmed me down), I would have busted down the door too.

I am going to make a note not to forget to enclose these funds, just so you know that I am actually, despite appearances, quite an upright citizen and unlike your son, I keep my promises.

And here's my other promise, and you are my witness: I promise to stop talking about this or thinking about it as of January 1. Maybe January 5. Hangovers always make me maudlin, so I'll give myself a few days. But I mean to stop going over this all, I really do. We weren't even married for that long. It's just that we were together for years and it all seemed pretty good, and then we got married and I thought, we'll grow into this, it's like the horizon you can see as you keep driving toward it, and then he got that grant and went away, and then within 3 months of a piece of paper, it's over.

One thing I do know is that you must not like me very much after my whole outburst last Christmas. And I really would like you to understand that I was a woman under pressure in ways I hope you never are, and to forgive me. I was in an altered state, in a riot of sudden heartbreak and—strangely—shame, Mrs. Watson. I felt shame, and maybe I had to physically lose my shit in order to have something to attach it to, if that makes any kind of discount, layman's psychoanalytical sense. I don't know why I felt shame except that I felt like such an idiot, a dumb fool. To find out it's all a lie, so quickly, like a slap in the face?

If you get a little mad at Josiah after the fact, if you can find it in yourself to let him know that you think he might have treated the whole situation, let alone me, a little better, that would be fine—

December 14, 1989

Dear Mrs. Watson,

I may have to start this letter all over again. I just got off the phone with my mother. I told her I was writing a letter to you.

I should tell you that she already thinks I'm nuts. She said that writing to you is a terrible idea. She said, Of all the ideas you've had, this one is probably the worst. By the way, she didn't think I was such a genius for marrying Josiah either. She'd said, I can't put my finger on it but he just seems so locked up.

I called her because I walked all the way home from work and the fresh air did absolutely no good at all. I still felt so pointless, like this small singular person among all this tinsel and present-buying and holiday window-dressing and women glowing in their men's arms, the frenetic lies of this awful season. So I called Mom, who can sometimes sharpen the point right back for me. Tonight on the phone I said, Mom—I really need to do this letter to Mrs. Watson because I feel I need to make amends. I need to just set things right, and then I can move on. And I feel bad for what I did to her house, and I'm really sorry, and she doesn't know.

Mom sniffed and told me, Honey, you have absolutely nothing to be sorry about.

But I broke her china, I told her.

He broke your heart, she said.

Mom, I really need to get the letter done, can you help me anyway?

With what? I'm no letter writer.

I'm just getting kind of derailed.

It's lose-lose trying to gain the sympathies of a mother-in-law in any situation, Mom said, let alone when she's only technically your mother-in-law because you can't bring yourself to sign the divorce papers that lout sent you. I heard that in Japan, young brides have to wash their mother-in-laws' feet.

I thought, maybe this is where I get the tangent reflex from. Certainly not Dad, who's straightforward as a two-by-four. I said, Mom, please? Whatever for Japan?

Start from the beginning, she said sensibly and went back to making her Thursday night lasagna.

So here goes.

In the beginning there was Josiah.

Junior year, Horace College. There appears in my History 201 class this 6' 5" transfer. Sandy blond. Watery gray eyes. Soft baritone voice. Long legs. Kind of graceful and not jockish. A tendency to tap his lip to consider a question before answering. Never interrupts. Never loses his temper even in the face of young Republicans. Is far and away more brilliant than any of us.

We flirt. We spend time. He says he quite enjoys my vivaciousness and curviness and I say I could climb him like a ladder to the stars. Chemistry, at this point. Besides I just escaped from a farce with a bass player named Boomer, and it is refreshing to be with someone whose general mindset is based on ideas, not amphetamines. Who cares more about injustice than shoes and is polite and does not lunge at me when I wear skirts. I think, I could not be safer with anyone.

Two, three years go by, there are ups and downs but I think this is called growing up, this is big-picture stuff. And I meet all of you, the blue bloods, get used to your ways: no raised voices, no interrupting, everything decent as dimity. I am by far the shortest and no good at those seasonal activities like iceskating and badminton, but I participate, I'm a good sport. I learn to eat your green jello molds with the ribbon of sour cream running through them. I learn to dab my mouth with the linen napkin at the table, politely, politely. I learn that in your house you don't really talk about things directly, you talk around them. Unless it's some kind of fabulous obvious accomplishment, such as Josiah's succession of academic awards, like the history medal he gets at graduation, which makes you get all teary-eyed, which I know because I am standing next to you, and I can hear every murmur, every sigh, as if you're watching your favorite movie, the one about the favorite son.

There is no romantic proposal but getting married makes sense, we decide. And the wedding is fun, a big musty banquet hall, the judge is an obese lady with a mustache, my mother cries like a fountain and runs her mascara and my father looks self-conscious but proud of himself in a suit. My family is kind of intimidated by your family but I think the years will go by and they will grow closer. Except there is one wrong note, when right before the ceremony, you come running into the dressing room where I'm setting the hair thing on my head, and you want to restyle my hair with a bunch of pins into something softer, and I refuse. I feel bad. But I don't want you to fuss over me. (Portents of future conflicts, though unrecognized. I am not good at the foresight, I admit. But I always wanted to apologize for that and never got to—how would I explain it? That I'm sorry if I was at all rude or ungracious but at that moment I felt like you were trying to prep me for some kind of patrician fertility ritual, and I couldn't deal?)

Married. Mr. and Mrs. Impellizeri-Watson—or at least that was the plan, but for some reason he never quite adds Impellizeri to his name. Whatever, I think, life is hectic, there's so much to do. We find a little apartment on Grand Street and get two cats, name them Vladimir Ittybit Lemon (Josiah names the tabby) and Splat (I name the white one), and have a few weeks. We make picnics on the fire escape, we toast the muggy nights. Then Josiah gets the telegram that he has been awarded an extremely prestigious grant to study for a year in Helsinki and Moscow. But it starts in the fall, less than three months away. But I certainly can't say, Don't go. And I have a job. I am working, so there is no question—I can't leave. And then he ships off all sorts of books and buys a hideous brown down coat and loads up this giant suitcase and is gone. I'll see you Christmas break, he says, I'll call, I'll write. *Dasvedanya.*

I do not remember one minute of September at all. I wake up in October and have grown this solitary skin. The apartment is intensely quiet, the air heavy and odd. I do not drink or smoke. I read a lot. I am careful to rein in my feelings and not flirt with that hunk down the hall. I try to eat lightly and be a good wife, despite a tendency to chafe, despite all that distance. I put on my glasses and think of him wearing his glasses in cavernous old libraries in Helsinki, in Moscow, wearing sweaters, his tartan scarf, poring over archives, learning, brain lit like a lamp. I come home from my job and sit by the phone most nights waiting for those faraway crackling calls, and read his letters, mostly laundry lists: what I did today without you.

But I think about how he'll come home and we'll wrap ourselves around each other and then head to your house for Christmas and show up at your door happy, and eat crackers and cheese in the living room and sing carols, and there will be that undersimmer of desire between us and the first time back in his arms will be electric. And I talk about it to Mom and Dad and they tell me they don't feel any sentimental twinge about skipping the holidays this year so that I can go be with Josiah and the Watsons, which makes me an emotional wreck but they tell me, Calm down, we'd rather eat Chinese anyway. And I think, Josiah will come home and we'll have two weeks, and then fueled on that he'll jet back to Helsinki and then it'll just be a quick four months and then he'll be back and then we can go on with our lives. Which means he will finish his great big thesis and no doubt get some kind of honor and we will embark on that part of our lives where we live where his first job is, maybe Kansas or Albuquerque, which will be fine because I can do anything I want, I can be a youngish wife in a new place with not too much expected of me, so I can make it up as I go along, and it will be fine.

And then Josiah calls to say he can't get a flight until Christmas Day. The phone line is clear, like he's talking through glass, like the idea of his being closer is actually making the phones better. Then, Christmas morning, oh my *gosh* he's coming home.

I drive to JFK in his vintage stickshift, that nemesis with the finicky clutch I can barely work. (My father says only academics and pretentious people drive stick shifts and never taught me.) But I get it in gear and drag-race the cabs on Northern Boulevard and hoot out loud inside the car and get there on time, shaking like a leaf, but I am there to meet him at baggage claim and there he is.

He is, it seems to me, a vertical study in haggard distractedness: a hug barely sustained, eyes on the departures board over my shoulder. The down jacket carries the scent of airplanes, of tobacco and moldy books.

Missed you, I say.

He puts his hand on my back. But it is not a possessive, sexy placement. It is more like a check, like *not now*.

Weird to be back, he says and his voice has this foreign, stilted cadence. Because when I get nervous I make jokes, and he had his hand on my back, I say, weird to be my back too. Which he doesn't get. He scans the airport's Santa display, an 8-foot-tall Santa riding a plane pulling a long line of enormous presents along the ceiling, like this insane galaxy of largesse is about to tumble down into the rotunda.

Wow, he says, but not in a positive way.

Duty free, I say, feeling like even those words have double, triple meanings, everything tumbling around in my brain at once.

Dah, he says.

You hungry? Did they feed you potatoes and borscht?

Running off at the mouth again. I thought he'd taken Aeroflot from Moscow, but it turned out he'd taken Finnair from Helsinki. He didn't tell me. I just feel so unwifely not knowing that. So you had ham on brown bread, I start—

Amy, he says. And he says my full name, not my nickname which he'd always used: *Aim*—as in, Aim true.

Clutch sounds kind of rough, he says as we start the frosty drive. And I have this heavy feeling, of heading away from safety. This is the first time I'm coming to your house as his wife. Will it be different? Will you be more welcoming? Not that you hadn't been, but I used to wonder if there wasn't just a note of bemused tolerance underneath your courtesy, your consideration, your always asking me about my family—*And how are your mother and father?* And your entire brood, the sons and daughters and spouses will all be at your antique clapboard house. And after me and Josiah not seeing each other for 3 months, maybe this is a bad idea.

So I start saying to Josiah that maybe we should have spent a day together first. Or he should have come back earlier.

I couldn't, he explains, rather shortly. I had to catalogue the univolumes.

To which I say, Of course. The univolumes. And then make a quip about unibrows, and then fumble my way back to small talk—how's your thesis, my job is the same, there's a new waitress at the coffee shop—wanting to say instead, *What* is this giant chasm between us? Is it not being together for months? Can we fix this please? Can you tell me how much you missed me so I don't feel like I'm talking to the glove compartment of your tiny old rattling car?

It is freeze-raining this flinty urban-looking stuff that softens into snow as soon as the lean New York highway trees turn into those larger, more spread out New England varieties. Venerable as opposed to scrappy. Better soil, I guess. And I say, Goodbye scrappy trees, and I am already feeling kind of spooked, jumpy, like maybe I forgot to eat or drank too much coffee. There are so many cars full of children, flashing hand signals and making faces out the rear windows, sticking out their healthy suburban tongues. I think, up in New England they just reproduce, whatever for the wife's career let's get more kids in the fields. And I'm sitting there watching Josiah drive, thinking, maybe I should relax and we can make a baby, and then he'll get back from his big year and I'll have a belly and then we'll—

I ought to just be fine with that, right? The same way I ought to be fine with how we got married in May and Josiah got his grant and flew away by September, leaving me with the apartment and parking the rattletrap stickshift and taking care of Vladimir and Splat and *assisting* him, as he'd asked me to—his words—with his *correspondence*.

But I realized that for those months, away from him, I had not exactly been fine. I never said it. But I refused to experience any sense of pleasure—as if there was some penance to do, or as if, since I hadn't wanted this, I wouldn't want anything else. I wondered what it would be like to be devoted to an academic with all my heart. To be devoted to someone who by nature lived in their own world, and whose ideas and pronouncements were vital to at least 50 to 100 people a semester. Not that there's anything wrong with that, but it is different. Like you, Mrs. Watson, devoted to Mr. Watson, who is preeminent in what? 17th-century English charters or something? But perhaps you struck his fancy as having an old-fashioned face and you blushed virginally at his attentions and he wrote you a little sonnet, and you still carry on this lovely private flirtation of verse and politesse. And he knows you are there—to cook for him, make him tea when he has to finish grading those final papers at 2 a.m., bear and feed and clothe and raise the children, who will look like him and make him proud—

In fact, I sensed, that was your field. No matter what you might have been interested in a long time ago, like French poets or missionary work, that was your field. And I'm not saying there's anything wrong with that but it feels, maybe, just to me, a little sad. Or not really sad, but it just brings up certain questions, like does a man have a field and a wife has a man? And so the man is supposed to be her field? And so the man sows his seeds in the field, et cetera?

The trees rolled by and the power lines scooped in motion to the highway, and Josiah said how great it was to be going home, meaning his ancestral, mom-and-dad home. Even though we had an apartment in Chinatown, lined floor to ceiling with milk crates of his books. And that in itself was telling. I was overwhelmed by telling feelings, but had no idea what they were telling me. So I chattered.

I said, I suppose my ancestral home, if I had one, would be the ice-cream parlor on Broadway and Maple in South Jersey, where my parents apparently fell in love over milkshakes, and since my grandparents came over in steerage on some foul steamship from the old country there is no real ancestral home left for them—or maybe some Umbrian field in Italy for Dad, some steppe in Poland for Mom.

There are no steppes in Poland, he said.

Then how do you get upstairs?

Silence. He was not entertained.

I know you take your history seriously, I said after a few minutes.

It's your history too, he said, and I felt like that was code for something, but what?

On I-90 we stopped for gas. I shut my eyes in the passenger seat and opened them, and saw this very tall man in a brown down coat walking around the car, his sandy blond hair rising off this ridged forehead. He rapped at my window. I rolled it down. He said, Do you have ten bucks for gas? All I've got are rubles and markkas.

I thought, it's my Josiah. He's come back.

I'd had these expectations of some romantic reunion, of love melting the very snow we trod on, of the tension of proximity, that delicious heat. I reached out the window with the money, he touched it. He got back in the car and I reached to touch his face. Remarkable. He turned and looked at me, and it was live, not phone or paper.

Hello, I said.

We should get going, he said.

My grandmother loves you for your genetic potential, I said.

What?

She wants the family to start getting taller and thinks you're the ticket.

And you?

I'm talking about her, I said. She just wants to be American. Like oval portraits in Virginia. She loves to show off our wedding pictures on her wall. My son-in-law, descended from the Mayflower, she tells her card-game ladies.

Hmm, he said as we pulled off the highway and into town. White picket fences undulated up and down hills. Historic houses stood well-decorated and comforting and imposing, set back from those fences, keeping their baronial distance. And I watched Josiah drive and tap his lip, that thin, George Washingtonesque lip.

By the time we pulled in the sun was going down like blood all over the snow. There was your house, the boughs festooning the porch columns, the golden hallway and the open door, everyone gathered to welcome us in, poinsettia trembling on the mantle, candles lit, tree adorned, siblings and spouses in red and white and green. And you, Mrs. Watson, were in that snow-white cardigan with the emerald edelweiss pin, and Mr. Watson was in his widewales and turtleneck, humming his hellos. And welcome, welcome, which is colder, Moscow or Helsinki? How was your fall? And a nice smile at me and a swift quizzical look as well, since I was wearing the right colors, but the wrong length—that velour minidress, forest green, and to set it off, red fishnet tights, and I know, these absurd Minnie Mouse red shoes. I'm sorry, I wanted to be sexy for Josiah, I forgot to be circumspect. The truth is I wasn't even wearing panties, I'd gone commando, thinking all sorts of slippery warm things. It had all made so much sense when I planned it. I said,

Oh, I'd so love to change. Capitulating. And you said, Well, why don't you two go upstairs then and unpack, and I'll get the goose out of the oven, and everyone oohed and aahed that we were having goose, so traditional, so Olde England, so fitting.

Shall I take you up in the attic with us? There isn't any sex, I can promise that. First we sat upstairs on that creaky old four-poster, surrounded by the stuff of his boyhood: all those records, piles of books, the encyclopedias he won in 6th grade, and the late '60s wallpaper you must have been drunk when you put up—those giant silver circles floating over that dusty brown sea. And since I hadn't seen him in months I was getting kind of hot (we're both women here, Mrs. Watson—you didn't bear all those children by eating cheese sandwiches), and I was thinking about what we could do with that four-poster. And he took my hand, and I jumped because there was a "listen" coolness to his skin as opposed to a "we just got here I haven't seen you in months let's do it quick before dinner" kind of heat. And I leaned into him reflexively *and he leaned away.*

I thought, if this goes on for too long I'm going to have to just jump him and break the ice. That is, after all, how I got him going in college. Anyway I pretended not to be too affected by his reticence. I began to fold some of his things to put them in the dresser like I always did when we came up here. I began to put our stuff around the room, a bottle of papaya and coconut lotion on the night table, hung my red silk scarf on the corner of the Clash poster. Usually the sight of that scarf kind of wakes him up—

And he said, I need to tell you something. I slept with some-one in Helsinki.

I must've not hung up the scarf securely, because it sud-denly fell off the corner of the poster and collapsed into a limp red heap on the fusty carpet.

And actually there was more to it than I said before. I re-member that you were calling *Five minutes* from downstairs.

And he said, No one else thought to do that kind of schol-arship but her, connecting the implications of the Irish famine of the mid-1800s with the rising pressure on localized Russian agrarian collectives.

And I said, Ah. So that's that what did it for you.

He forgot who he was talking to. He was getting carried away. He said, Well, in a way—

And then saw my face, a blank stone, and clammed up.

No, I lied. I really want to know.

Well, he said. Anyway, I told you.

Yes you did, I said. My ears were ringing. There was a dead thing on the rug, oozing from the single gunshot, the coup de grace. I thought of our cats, about to be parsed out.

You can take Vladimir, I said. But Splat is mine.

Of course I can't take care of anything, he said. I'll have to return to Helsinki, and then when I come home, we can make the—

Arrangements.

Of course I'm returning there so soon, he said.

Feebly I said, I guess we can wait.

You're very quiet, he said.

I'm sure I'll make some noise later, I said.

We sat there, the air between us buzzing and folding in on itself. Then he said, I'm sure they're waiting for us downstairs. Mum made that goose.

Duck duck goose, I said, thinking, that's the *last* time I ever make light of anything for Josiah ever, ever, ever.

And just like that, our marriage opened up like a sinkhole and disappeared.

December 16, 1989

Dear Mrs. Watson,

I had this revelation yesterday, over my third cup of black coffee at the coffee shop. The waitress has decided to stop talking to me and just fill the cup, and every once in a while she says, Long letter, and I say, Mother-in-law, and she says, I never talked to mine even when she was mine. So you see, it's good that I'm making this gesture. And I was thinking about there being this connection between us all—the ones whose marriages crashed and burned no matter how ornate the wedding, or how simple or how careful each person was to be nice or not—when a girl walked into the coffee shop. She made a splash in the dingy place. She gave off a scent of some musky, spicy perfume, had gleaming earrings—a long-haired exotic looking girl a few years younger than me, with a swarthy face and a hook nose. And she was on the arm of a blond whitebread guy who was dutifully carrying her bohemian-looking bookbag and hanging on her every thrilling word.

And I realized this: I may not come from a long line of witches, but I suspect that part of my appeal to Josiah was a muted version of that, a covert suggestion contained in my dark hair—of swirling gypsy skirts, those swarthy types who chewed on silver coins and divined the future in a cup of tea. And maybe once he actually experienced the genuine Russian article, my mystique lost its appeal. But again, it's a little late, this is all a rehash. I may have wondered this in a tiny little nightlight of an idea some night when we were still together and he'd just rolled over to go to sleep, and let it go, and now look.

And then last night, thinking of how Josiah might have suddenly understood the folly of his little fantasy with me, or even suddenly realized he was bored, and whatever else he realized, or didn't, and just went and did her anyway, I just had to cut loose. And I had a lot of loose to cut because writing this letter is letting all the ghouls out of the crypt. So I went over to the hunk's apartment down the hall and I said, I give up, let's do it. He didn't hem or haw or frown or consider or analyze. He said—and this was music to my ears—I've got protection.

So we did it against the wall and on the couch, on the floor, over the coffee table, and he likes to do it from the back, and he has a really thick, meaty cock, and the skin of it for some amazingly exotic reason is grayish blue, and I watched it go in and out (I am flexible, Mrs. Watson), and I came like a banshee. I have not been this turned on since high school, when me and the kinky Puerto Rican kid from trigonometry class used to freak out in his bedroom. And years ago, back in college when I met Josiah and he said, I hate the idea of women as packages, I thought, well not everyone is a voyeur, is a clown, it's all right—but just to see if I could get a rise out of him (pun intended), I would dress up in some of my old getups from high school, my sleek black pumps from the uptown cha-cha store and this garter thing I bought in Alexander's, just to kind of spice things up, and he would come home from his day at the library and walk into the bedroom where I'd have carefully displayed myself like living pornography on the bed, and he'd just go, Oh.

Oh.

I was the Jezebel invader, the whore sent by the devil. I was so embarrassed, felt a film of dirt coating my skin, questioned why I could even think that being that crass was appealing, how base, how common, how cheap I made myself—and why would I have to do that to get off anyway?

I used to think that Josiah wasn't into freaky stuff because he found it kind of tricky ethically, like to be nasty was not to respect women or something, and I did try to appreciate that, the PC aspect of eschewing role play or rough stuff for something more utopian and democratic and equal.

The last time I tried to get all tarted up, he said, How come you do that to yourself?

What I would do to myself if I could, I thought. But I resolved to give up the black lace, to keep my voice down (not like I'm a shrieker but hey, when the spirit moves), to not threaten, to aspire to something more platonic but still erotic. But when it came right down to it, Josiah went to another ice-cream store anyway. Good old vanilla with a Russian cherry on top, a surly vodka-soaked Soviet bloc cherry. So what kind of respect is that?

So last night, just to be sure I was really letting go, I said, Hey, hold on, and I threw on a towel and ran back down the hall and searched the floor of my closet until I found those old evil sisters. I slipped them on my feet and tottered back in— and *boom*. Not, *Oh*. Hunk is half-Jamaican, half-Jewish and he is built like a truck and plays the drums, so his shoulders and pectorals—the latter being a word I wouldn't even touch with aristocratically narrow Josiah—are like mountains you can climb. This guy is old-fashioned, no-holds-barred, rear-wheel drive, —what a *mechanism*. And he knows all these positional tricks: put a pillow under the ass for traction, for g-spot targeting, all that, and he is younger than me and he is quiet and even polite and even kind of studious, and was raised by his mother and sisters in the Southwest in a genuine adobe house and is *not* a de facto heir of the Western patriarchy that just helps itself to whatever it wants.

And he has never even been to Massachusetts and can't name any of the Pilgrims and thought the ship they came in on was called the *Wallflower*.

And received much physical gratitude from me for that.

Soon after Josiah's bomb drop, maybe two weeks later, Josiah and I had a conversation that went like this:

I just called to say Happy New Year, he said.

You too. Don't Russians have a different New Year?

No, not since 1698, as far as I know.

Where are you?

Paris. We just decided to escape, for a week, maybe. Just a week.

We. That was fast.

Well—

You sound like a Russian talking English.

It soaks in, he said, it's amazing. But I wanted to tell you something. I wanted to tell you that I didn't plan this. It just happened.

Happened.

I was not looking for it.

But you didn't stop it.

No, I didn't. But I didn't go out looking for it.

So it was like, fate that caused this all to happen?

Sure, kind of. We were just at a party, neither one of us expected—

Two speak as one.

But I didn't intend—and to tell you the truth I thought you might have something really clever to say about it. One of those Amyisms.

Whatever on that. And you're not sorry.

Well, no. I mean, you seemed pretty mad about it when I told you, so—

And therefore that was a sign you should continue?

You're getting this all mixed up, Aim.

You kept seeing her because I lost my shit over Christmas?

Well, no, but, I suppose if you'd wanted to work things out—

How?

Aim, let's not. I just wanted to say *S Novym Godom*!

What?

Happy New Year.

Amy, he said, because I was quiet.

What? I said. And what's her name? Does she look like your mother? Are you going to marry her and reproduce and have adorable hybrid kids? Or is she already pregnant and that just happened too? I never expected that you were the infidelity type, you know? You got me with that one.

Amy.

Don't Amy me. Do you know how hard I was trying to be good while you were gone? Do you know how good I was? Like a princess in a storybook, waiting for her prince to come home, just up there in her tower, devotedly, foolishly. What an asshole I was.

Hey. Let's not go there. That's old history already.

History!

And I knew I'd lost all self-control there. Forfeited my position. And in fact that was true, as he wrote later in a letter that I burned quickly and decisively. He said my "little outburst was the proverbial straw that fractured the back of the camel." Which was, he explained, a translation of the Russian interpretation of the English colloquial, which he found far more realistic and better suited for use.

So is this Russian love of his. For Josiah, clearly, it is far more realistic and better suited for use.

Maybe that's what happens if you never talk about stuff. Maybe an impressionable young boy inclined to not look too deeply inside himself might grow up to think it was possible that stuff just *happens*. You just *happened* to fall into bed. But not even weather or the rising and falling of stars just happens. There is always a process. There is a spark, and smoke, and then eventually, if you give it enough air, a flame. Then the house burns to the ground.

When a mother treats her son like a prince, maybe she accidentally convinces him that his impulses belong to the category of divine rights. And it is dawning on me that it was so convenient for Josiah to tell me about his sleeping with someone else when and where he did. Christmas, we're together six hours, we're at his parents' house, physically we are up in the attic above an entire family of happy couples in deep holiday mode.

He was counting on the fact that I would not freak out.

Why? Was he assuming I wanted to fit in so badly that I would just pretend everything was lah-de-dah and be fine and behave?

Maybe he thought I would do it for his sake, because after all he hadn't been home in so long, and wouldn't it be awful to waste the precious hours of his return to the bosom of the family on a scene?

Or maybe I was persona non famiglia, so what does it matter? Maybe he'd rationalized that he was never entirely sure of me anyway but just didn't know, and now that he had found his true love—who would dance naked under the northern lights for him, but in a nonaggressive way—he just didn't care?

Or most likely he was assuming he'd tell me and then since we were both so well-educated and civilized we'd wait until we were alone to discuss it.

Alone when? He was not going to come back to the city with me, was he? He was going to stay up there in the protective blue-blood bosom of his family while I limped home to my suddenly totally empty situation—though it had been empty for months already, I just mistakenly thought it was still occupied.

Which I why I have changed Vladimir's name. He is now officially Elvis Impellizeri. Hunk thinks it's cute. Elvis and Splat Impellizeri. Sounds like hoodlums, he said.

Hood-looms, it sounds like.

Hunk has a slight accent from going to school for a year in London. He is not a dolt. He says I should sign the papers when I feel like signing the papers and let my Waspy ex twist in the wind. He says the timing probably has to do with a green card. He says, And why are you giving his parents money a year later when they're lucky you didn't go out and key his car? And he says, What's the big deal anyway, you guys didn't turn each other on, you like the jungle and he likes the steppes.

Whoa, I said. Say that again?

You like the hot, the moist, the intense, the red, the black. He likes his jones on the loftier side.

You're a *drummer?*

And he was all into sitting in front of a book for a year straight, and you seem to like to mix your brain with your body, so enough already, right?

And I realized, right. And here's the thing: I buried what I was afraid of, that feeling of being trapped in the wrong picture, right at my feet. Maybe Josiah could smell it wafting up on certain damp days, like when I was extra frustrated or crying. Maybe the smell of my doubts came up right out of the ground. Maybe he was discouraged by this. And so he sought his own comforts.

This is the truth—I used to love going to your big saltbox colonial at 14 Shire Road. How picturesque and charming. So opposite from my parent's squat little ranch house with the topiary hedges and the cast-iron lawn set that pretty much screams *I love you New Jersey but it's time to redecorate.* And I loved that you took the trouble to research how many windowpanes the place originally had, and came up with 12. Which Mr. Watson tried to explain to me was so important to preserve the house's colonial heritage. So you should all have 12 sections too, I joked. This is reproduction 18th-century seed glass, he continued. And of course I found something funny in that—you know, men, seed—and he gave me a what-are-you-on look, and then we changed subjects with a nice glass of scotch, and he said, Not many girls I know drink scotch, as if he were still 21. And maybe then he had an inkling of what his son might see in this curvy little wife, although he was a little late.

But the problem is that I do not see how someone could be turned on by a man you have lived with for 30 years, who decides that the status quo affords him some rights, and so doesn't really have to make an effort to be attractive, and that his stature as a great thinker—capital G capital T—should be the best aphrodisiac, and therefore doesn't always brush his teeth, and hums through those great twin caverns in his skull, hums a different classical masterwork than what he is blasting in the living room on that pretentious German stereo. And wears a rumpled mustard-colored bathrobe and black socks around the house. And has this flat, flat ass, probably from being flattened on the flat seat of that 18th-century spindle-back chair he sits in for 10 hours at a stretch. I mean where's the virility in that?

Maybe I was thinking, this is Josiah in 30 years, and therefore this is me, stuck in some university town with this rumpled scion in my bed, bad breath but brilliant, and I am supposed to just make his tea and admire? And get the kids to school in the morning so he can read the paper and keep up with the current events in his field?

Because if it were me? I would eat my young. Not literally, but I would be that lunatic professor's wife who drives too fast and drinks too much cheap wine at the receptions. And when my husband is feted for yet another accomplishment I have an embittered edge to my toast, hissing, Yes, here's to my *brilliant* husband. And regarding my children, I would quietly deconstruct their egos for playing their own insidious part in the trap called domesticity with Josiah. And so it wasn't going to work, and therefore why should I even care that he slept with someone in Helsinki and our marriage went to hell?

And therefore I should just sign the papers, which sit in their administrative envelope, insidious, powerful, taking over the apartment.

There are different categories for getting a divorce. You can cite neglect or abuse. You can cite adultery. I guess at some point last spring, when I was asked if I wanted to file the papers, I said hah, I couldn't be bothered wasting my time, and so Josiah did. And the box he checked as the reason we were seeking the first stage of divorce, a *separation agreement*—two words that do *not* belong together—was "irreconcilable differences."

I objected. I said, That's not why. Why is because you left me for this harlot in Helsinki.

She's not a harlot, he said, so gallantly.

It's not a matter of our having differences. It's because you fucked someone else.

Which is because we had differences, he said, which really blew me away. Because he had never once said anything like, Hey, we need to talk. Although I should have understood this—in your family, Mrs. Watson, the stuff you talk about is all okay. It's the stuff you *won't* talk about.

If we didn't have differences, he said, I wouldn't have gone astray.

Cute, I said. Blame the victim.

Josiah left behind his vodka collection, which I am now

sampling, and about 12 crates of Russian books, which I have donated to the woman who runs command central from her shopping cart on the Bowery. She now believes she has the key to world peace, or at least knows how to communicate with the spies, who are everywhere. In basements, she said. In attics.

Yes, I said. Definitely in attics.

What is irreconcilable is how that whole fall I was in our little apartment in Chinatown, dutifully going to my job and pining for Josiah and thinking that when he got back I'd be so nice to him, I'd cook Russian stews to ease his culture shock. And you were being a nice mother-in-law and sending me recipes for his favorite dishes (actually he told me he hates squash au gratin and please, do yourself a favor and forget that jello mold). While I was rationalizing everything—just because he tunes out so much doesn't mean he doesn't care, he'll call, he'll call—do you know what? Your angelic scholar wunderkind with the gray eyes and the sandy hair and the long, long legs you so maternally adore was indeed on his research grant in Moscow and Helsinki. And he was indeed meeting the academic requirements of that prestigious grant, the one that bestows its recipient with a stature like a knighthood in some circles. He was, in fact, meticulously "cataloguing the great McKenzie Slovenia archives, while simultaneously addressing future implications for the Molotov-Ribentropp debacle." He had thought it such a bold stroke to actually describe it as a debacle instead of a pact—to add that editorial note, as he called it, with a bold flourish.

It was a bullshit pact, he'd said somewhat bluntly for such a usually refined, restrained, impartial discusser of the human tide, which of course made me happy since I thought it was a sign of red-blooded passion that would of course be availed on me. And on that exalted grant, after he had done his requisite 8 hours in the archives, he'd get a tap on his shoulder and look up and there was the bony homewrecker, waiting to take him to her Soviet bloc apartment, where he could thrill her with his gallantry, where I suppose she made sure to present herself scantily wrapped in some peachy, pastel, nonthreatening confection. *That* is irreconcilable.

A debacle, not a pact.

Hunk says, I'm taking you to breakfast. We go to the coffee shop, where the morning waitress is wearing a Santa hat. She had just gotten used to the fact that there is no more lanky blond husband around, wedged into his book while I try to chatter. Now she winks and gives me a thumbs-up behind Hunk's back.

December 20, 1989

Dear Mrs. Watson,

Even though I am going to have to go back over my letters and pick and choose the parts to send you, I want you to know that in all of them, I had the best of intentions. I wanted to set the record straight on what happened, and show myself to not be a shrill and annoying stranger but a girl with a heart, who loved your son, even though we were not really a great match, but nevertheless did not misbehave, at least until the night after I got home from last Christmas, although then I went nun for months, which Hunk said at breakfast he could tell. He said, you take a while to uncurl.

If a while is an hour, I said.

He likes his bacon crispy, his eggs scrambled. Whereas Josiah liked boiled eggs, something I could never stand, the sulfur smell always making me want to gag. And he ate his bacon limp, which I felt was somehow unmanly, but he said he'd never had it any other way, there was never time with 4 kids to wait until the bacon got crisp—you'd miss the bus to school.

Hunk is a slow eater. He *savors*. He also likes my red Minnie Mouse shoes despite their toes being dented, scars from that panicked night last year. And I won't even mention how tender fingers can be through fishnet. And he finds that green velour dress the cat's meow—he ran his hand along it like a hand through kittycat fur and I purred. And I feel like I am going through some kind of married woman's reawakening, after trying so hard to lock myself into the straitjacket of fidelity, and for what?

And maybe Josiah was going through this too, up near the thatched roof of the world. And maybe I should have a little more sympathy. My mother says chemistry, not biology, comes first. Then biology, she says, looking saccharine at Dad. Spare me, I say. But there is something about being dewy, and female. About being in love. I guess I was trying, and hoping we'd kind of grow together, or at least in the same direction, like trees on a hill—up, spreading our branches into each other—

Meanwhile, this Russian rimjob Korsakov, is she living at your house?

December 22, 1989

Dear Mrs. Watson,

This morning over breakfast I realized that I have veered off course a little, but now I'm back. And it feels good to get back to the point and to be writing to you, and I hope you're doing well. In my effort to paint myself in your reticent eyes as no Amy Evil, I would like to pick up at your dinner table, pre-storm.

Did I know it would be the last one? By the time I sat down to eat with all of you? I guess I wasn't sure. Josiah naturally wouldn't really look at me and instead was making all sorts of chatter with his sisters, who were so curious about his travels and kept glancing at me briefly as I tried not to glower. (Is it that you are all so well read, Mrs. Watson, that they say things like *travels*? Is that from your reading them 19th-century books when they were little kids? Maybe there are all sorts of messages tucked into those little stories that they soaked up like little sponges.)

The roast goose sat in the center of the table, a hurt and glistening creature, hot juices sizzling off those blistering lumps of potato. And that nerdy son-in-law of yours said, Well Mrs. Watson, you sure cooked that goose. He was referring to that line, *your goose is cooked*, which of course he didn't know how to say, because he's too busy breathing all that earnest environmentalist air. But everyone chuckled congenially. Congenitally. And meanwhile of course a phrase like your goose is cooked had special meaning to me, suddenly, awfully.

I know in your family people do not make a scene. Especially during one of your archetype Christmas family dinners. But I sat there, among you all, and I felt like a Martian, like it was all a farce—Josiah smiling and chatting as if nothing had happened, and me emptied of blood, realizing that I was present at a profound and roaring contradiction. And there was just something about the stillness of those creamed pearl onions and baby peas in their porcelain serving dish, and the obedient settings of heirloom silver (was it really made by Paul Revere for your *cousin*?) laid along the crisp white tablecloth like virgins for sacrifice, and that poor neckless goose, and the muddy gravy in the ironstone gravy boat, lumps of fat scumming up the top. And then there was the stalwart perfection of the way Mr. Watson carved that goose and held the slices aloft, and your adoring looks at him, and all of us voicing our admiration, our approval, watching, behaving, people making jokes about how Maria, not Mareeah, was eating for two as she nestled another generation of upperclass New England ease in her belly, and then that clever little toast about *whom* (not who) ever might be next, and then we got to hear everyone else's big news as we went all around the table—We know now it's a boy—We're putting a bid on a house—We set a wedding date.

And I wanted to get up and say, And *we're* getting a divorce.

Josiah, your gifted one with the endless brain and legs and arms, and me, his odd little New Jersey firecracker wife that you never really got, with the curly hair and too much eyeliner and the platform boots and the forest green velour minidress, are getting a *divorce* because he got lonely or inspired or just horny, and went after some Soviet tail on a cold night and now he thinks his future lies between those pale white legs and maybe it does.

I remember I was drowning in my own hellish reverie when someone touched my arm. And it wasn't Josiah, it was you, Mrs. Watson, politely rousing me so you could ask me to pass the peas. Actually, if you were willing to reach across me you could have gotten the peas yourself. But there are rules to follow, aren't there? And then you asked me to pass the peas. Amy? you said, Could you? Please? And so on and so forth and then there was gravy on the mirror and the look on your faces and I ran out the room down the hall past all those disapproving books and the classical music endlessly noodling out of the stereo and fled out the door where it was 18 nipple-hardening New England degrees.

Remember, I am enclosing money to cover the damage. It will be in the envelope. So if my finances permit, I will enclose another $20 to cover the cost of repairing the dents in your front door. I had honestly forgotten about that part, when I realized it wouldn't hurt to kick the hale, oak front door to your house, and just decided it would be fine to take some frustration out on that well-hewn panel since I was wearing platform shoes I'd probably burn as soon as I got home, right before I climbed into the lost and found box and waited for someone to come and pick me out.

Tired of kicking, I sat on the porch for a long time. No one came out. Especially not Josiah—using inertia like a weapon, really. There were so many times he could have said something, like how about back in September, when he'd just arrived in Helsinki and we already had this awkward raw empty thing on the phone. Or was he too busy watching himself with his third analytical eye, the eye that looks at every single human interaction and sees a possible historic trend, to realize, *Shit, this is real, I just had this wild vodka-soaked night of passion with this total Russian academic babe, I'd better call my wife*? And then it went on, night after night, until he thought, *It's too late, I'll tell her when I see her*, and let himself roll onto his cheap Russian harpie again.

After I'd locked myself in your attic, and redistributed Josiah's things all over the room, I had this moment of complete calm. And it all became clear. I had to get out. The house itself, which had protected and sheltered all of you, was as much a problem as Josiah himself. But the attic door would not open. And I guess that's when I started to scream.

It was the firemen who got me out of your house, finally. Using very careful language so as not to upset me (I imagine this is in some manual: *How to not make it worse*), they asked me if I could just tell them, through the door, if I was hurt. And had I hurt myself? I thought, in another moment of clarity, that if I said yes, that would require a whole different set of forms and possibly a psych evaluation. I said no. In fact I hadn't thought of hurting myself.

By not trying to talk me through undoing the lock, by opting instead to bust the door down, the firemen let me know that they cared about me. They did not want to take any chances. And I am sure they were all weighing their options—if we don't bust in and get her, we could be here all night, and miss Christmas entirely. Even though those men were the ones stuck in the firehouse on duty, one did tell me that his wife was on her way over with a fruitcake, and he couldn't wait to see her. He said to me, That's what a good marriage is—when your wife comes to bring you a fruitcake Christmas night, and instead of getting mad at you for working, is happy you were able to get time-and-a-half. That is so real, I thought, sitting in the back of that truck with the blanket around my shoulders. It is so much more real than this vague but hopeful abstraction I had with Josiah.

It was snowing a little—giant, separate, poodle-y flakes. The firemen stood around like a team after a scrimmage and they said, We didn't know if you were all right or not. They were still somewhat out of breath, still jazzed from their effort. They said, with no irony whatsoever, Our job is to keep you safe.

It is a wonderful feeling, I said, knowing that someone out there wants to keep me safe.

Miss, they said. Of course. And hopefully there is someone else who wants to keep you safe too. And then one of them nodded.

And I think I burst into tears and asked them to just take me with them, anywhere, somewhere else, and then one asked, Are they hurting you? And of course that would have been awful and if I'd said yes I would have been vindictive and selfish in a way you may have thought I was. But of course I am not. I am, I think, incapable of such calculations. So I said no, of course not.

Of course not, one said. And another said, take care of yourself. Each one of them looked more Irish, more salt-of-the-earth New England-style, than the next. Those thick lashes, blue eyes, the Irish overbite thing, shoulders thick with rescue strength. They stood around, lingering, making sure I was okay. As inside your historic home, to be honest, you were taking care of your own.

And you were quite willing to look the other way while a spirited girl with curly hair and triangular thighs voluntarily allowed her husband to slowly cut off her air supply at the rate of perhaps 20 percent a year. Can benign neglect be reinterpreted as subtle abuse? I would say so.

What does she look like?

I wish I could call you up and ask you that. Have you seen her? You must have. My guess is that he wants to marry her and bring her here and get her the green card and she has promised him in a sly but Eastern-bloc, desperate-under-the-surface way that she will be grateful for life. But I know when I called, you'd be standing in your kitchen, making that, *Well, I never* face at Mr. Watson while you humored me on the phone, and probably there's a roast in the oven and that dog of yours is licking his balls by the trash bin, or maybe he's been exiled to the back porch for taking a piss on the refrigerator again, which is why people neuter their dogs.

And I completely understand that in-laws don't really have anything to do with divorce papers. But with this divorce I also lose you. Or leave your sphere. I will not be one of your son's wives or your daughter's husbands sitting up at the holiday table waiting to pass Mr. Watson the pie. And why does this matter at all? I was a face in your life, Mrs. Watson. And maybe—although you no doubt crossed me off—if I can just offer my side of the story you might just look again.

So I'm sorry about screwing up your Christmas last year. And I'm sorry about screwing up my last Christmas at your house. As I think I said before, I'd like to finish this letter, or at least the parts of it I want to send you, before I go see my parents in New Jersey for the holidays and shine my high-intensity lamp upon them, as Mom says. I know she loves me, though. She says, I can never keep up with you, but when you find what you're looking for, I think you'll slow down.

I say, Mom, anyway, what am I looking for? A husband? Because that didn't work so well.

And she shrugs. I don't think so, she says. I don't even think it's about Josiah's mother. You just *think* you want her to forgive you.

She's not just Josiah's mother, I say. There's more to her than that.

There's more to all of us, she says.

We are wrapping presents when this conversation takes place, something I mention because my mother's version of wrapping presents is to smash a roll of wrapping paper around a box and then rope it into submission with an entire spool of silver curling ribbon, and then add at least three clashing, pre-stapled bows. Which I missed last year, and I'm glad I'm not missing again. Because she admitted to me that having Chinese food last year was not exactly festive, and she would prefer to *not* do that anymore.

Wrapping presents also involves the consumption of extremely fattening Christmas petit fours from the local bakery, Susie's Snowflake. There is nothing snowy or flakey about anything that Susie makes. The petit fours could double as hockey pucks.

Why am I telling you this? It's *life*, Mrs. Watson.

So my mother pops in a petit four, then zips the scissor blade down the curling ribbon, which tightens into an insane, curlicued mess. There, she says. Lovely. But I still think you need something.

Again with the tangents, I say.

No, really. She looks at me, and I can see my eyes in her eyes. You need something, she says. But maybe you just need to stop looking so hard for it. And then maybe it will come to you. That's what I think.

As soon as I can figure out what you're talking about, I'll try it, I say.

Please use the money in this envelope (or, really, in the envelope which will hold the letter when I get a chance to rewrite it into its final, readable form), to fix your house. Hire someone to get last year's stains and scum out of the dining room already. Get some nice handsome carpenter to fix your attic door, which I am sure is still off the hinges—probably just propped against the attic wall, where it was placed in the aftermath of my departure. I can see you and Josiah, up in the attic where it looks like a hurricane hit, as you carefully try to find a place for that poor door. And you settle on the wall, and then find its balance so it doesn't swing over and crash to the floor and make an awful noise and wake little Washington. I can see that pretty clearly, actually. But it doesn't bother me anymore.

TREMOR

It's Easter: my grandmother sits on the edge of our couch, cake plate on her lap, fork balanced on the side. I sit close as I can without touching, breathing in her cologne as she talks. A voice full of inflections, heavy on the first syllables, sweet as the jam she serves inside hot pancakes, apricot, sugared. I swing my legs back and forth and watch my shoes fly over the rug, the black patent-leather cars of an amusement ride. I imagine sitting inside them and holding onto the cross-straps, tall as my ankle, feeling the wind. Grandma's talking, she's watching Grandpa, she's watching my father, my father's her son.

Grandpa Will isn't my father's father, but Daddy calls him Pop. He's hunched over the cake plate at the table, rushing each forkful before the crumbs have time to fall. My mother keeps the house clean, *immaculate* is what my father says, you're either too careful or not careful enough. Good cake, Verna, Grandpa's saying to Grandma. He says, Voiner, and she says, I didn't make it. She's taught me this: a compliment is only a compliment if you say thank you, an answer is always an answer even if it's not what you want to hear. My mother gets up to straighten the Easter flowers on the mantel, she moves the vase over to the center from the side.

Daddy gets out the Polaroid camera, my favorite since I get to hold the blank squares and watch them turn into pictures. Here we go, he says, aiming, and Grandpa sits up, brushes the shoulders of his navy blue suit, straightens the union clip on his tie. He smiles, crooked teeth, he looks at Grandma. Verna, he says. Verna, let Jack get a picture. Give Grandpa something, he'll try to give it to Grandma.

Counting sixty to myself I walk around the room with the new picture, which will look like this: Grandma in her gray dress with the Chinese collar, her silver hair fluffed around her face, only slightly taller standing than her seated Will. It will be crisp and bright and centered, and they'll both be smiling; my father is a professional and he started young. First shots with a Box Brownie camera: overcoats on a diagonal, neighbors on a tilting porch, 1938, 1939, 1940, Bronx. In my hand the Polaroid turns bright, and in it Grandpa's squinting a little as he looks up at Grandma, but Grandma's head is just a blur.

Funny, says my mother, with free film you never know. Daddy gets packages all the time, yellow boxes in wrapping that pops when I press it, cameras packed in white macaronis that float in my bath. Grandma goes back behind Grandpa and leans over his shoulder. Is this good? She grips the top of his chair for support, and he folds his repairman's hands on one leg. My father waits a minute after looking through the camera. Paprika, he says. Don't move, but say paprika. When they do he clicks the shutter and Grandma laughs.

There, my mother says. More coffee? Grandpa's already asking Grandma. I hold the milky snapshot cupped in my hands. It's already got outlines, the splash of light from the lamp on the wall, Grandpa's dark shoe. I count way up to fifty-four, fifty-five, the color's flushing in, fifty-nine—

Show me first, Daddy says.

I whisper, Why is it still blurry around her head?

Just keep her company.

All the rest of the afternoon I watch her. She fits four fingers into the handle of the china cup. She takes sips, she doesn't gulp. When she sits up I can see how the belt wraps around her waist, its buckle shaped like a tiny leaf. She sits with her feet together, the soles of her white sandals are cream-colored and thick, the pin she's wearing is a painted flower, her lips are a soft red. Sometimes she shakes her head as if thinking, No, not today. Sometimes. Most of the time. Her head shakes all by itself.

My father's camera is what found out first. After they've gone, he lays the pictures out and we look at the blurry contours, the motion that makes Grandma look like she's just heard a strange sound or decided to leave the room. I'll take more pictures, he says, with a flash and a faster camera, I want to get in between when it stops and it starts. I'm sent into the kitchen to wash the Easter plates from my stepstool, I do each one slowly until it comes out all white. The water sloshes, the soap makes bubbly hills in the corners of the dishpan, Grandma blurs in the car as Grandpa drives them home, all the way up to Parkchester. It's not uphill, my mother's told me, you just say up. But I still see it like that.

PERFORATED: A LEXICON

August In August I did not have this problem. It was brought on by saltwater in the September sea, then by standing with the dog in the rain worrying, I was worrying, the dog was worrying, the rain was worrying, I forgot to go inside, caught a cold

Baby Tiny face with hole punched through it, rimmed in indignant red

Book Young man's diatribe made into seven-figure deal made into chunk of paper and ink 6 by 8 by 1 made into movie. Mom says, Don't you know who he is? No? He is so much younger than you. Maybe you should try to emulate him instead of those Slavic loner poets? You haven't been writing? What's wrong with your ear? You can tell me. You don't know? Haven't you gone to a doctor? What are you waiting for? I never like to wait, but I know you two like to try herbal teas first, but stay away from rose hips, they can kill you

Cape Cod We'd wanted just to escape. It's so catalogue, the in-laws' shingled cottage. But the land, the land is a fear-biter: poison ivy lurks like a secret where you step. Labradors pant from the toxins of ticks. Lawns groan and lust for bogs. Crows bicker low in the trees, saltwater lodges in the ear and refuses to come out

City The only way to love you is to not be with you. The streets are ringing, the buildings are ringing, the power lines vibrate, the sidewalks spark

Cold No slap across the head, no sudden explosion, no sonic boom, no hot slag of metal slammed into skin, just a common cold neglected too long, an infection that nestled against the eardrum and slowly ate through it, stoned caterpillar at the mushroom, and now here we are

Doc Long ago forgotten, the cross-country runner who had nothing to say, whose legs spoke instead, articulating miracles, tendons flexing into sonnets beneath the knee. I always preferred that language, that clarity of physical words, now he's the lab coat in the exam room, now he's explaining, 50 percent there, 50 percent gone, I can't believe it's you, you look great except for that ear

Drum Membrane stretched over the tiny bones it can't catch the sounds right, vibrates and flutters and chatters in hollow tones, complaining of its own failure, making it worse, howls into the inner sanctum, can't stop calling its own name

Ear The bones: tiny gloves that catch sounds in their taut palms and toss them to the next player, all in silence except for those sounds. The canal: a vacuum, normally, a mute factory peaceful as heaven, a cult of pale workers who never speak. But now they're all rioting, it's bedlam, it's panic, an anthill under a boot

Fame The renowned lobster tank in the fabulous coffee shop on the corner uptown, tank's cloudy water and all, where everyone comes to have their picture taken with Louie the combover king, who takes a break from his gladhanding to tell me, Young lady, your phone is ringing, can't you hear it? Are you hard of hearing?

Fix And there is no turning back, except for going under, having them sew in there, dig into the delicate waxen interior, spirals and jetties of the soft shell's inside. And maybe it works, maybe not, and the chances are, and the percentages are. Not exactly foolproof, they say, as if a fool should be allowed anywhere near the inside of the head, in the secret place where air pours through and rings into the brain

Girl Forty-two heading for forty-three like a crash-test car, headlong with no choice

Grief The silver pendant hanging low across the chest reads *I wish I could hear you better*. Goodbye quiet and lovely thoughts, born in the safety of the white box, delivered intact and hearable. Hello renegade frequencies, the radio dials wheeling, reverberations, hums, clicks

Grudge For lunch I have a dirt sandwich, every day. Your fault. Had I not gone swimming, had you not accused me of never wanting to dip into the waters of life

Guitar Angels come down with snow-white wings and coal dust on their faces, and ruined lungs embering behind the ratty bibs of overalls. Can't hear to tune it, this infernal ringing, the rains are coming down immortally, constantly, but it's not raining. There is a hole in your eardrum the shape of an f-hole in an old acoustic, the doc says, you have no choice but to respect it, you have a hole in your head

Hat Equals lifesaver: to prevent a drop of rain from entering the ear, passing through the perforated eardrum and into the brain, potentially fatal

Heart Racing, chased by caffeinated dogs, the cotton ball fell out of the earlobe while I was in the shower, am I dead?

Hesitation A foot hovering on the threshold of the escalator, picturing shredded clothes, balance a byproduct of intact eardrums and therefore the inverse, the ringing uncertainty

Hope In tiny bottles set on a sunny window, now gathering dust along with the light

Ing Oh, the endless ing of it all. Not a ring with a beginning and an end. A ringing, a yawning middle of ringing, flat and endless as an ocean. An ocean-ing. Not a hunger. A hungering. So hungry for quiet, for white rooms and mother's lullabies, sweetly heard, sugar spun. Not a need to hear. A need to be hearing. I can't be hearing you, it's too noisy. Could you be being quiet and saying it again?

Money The boulevard roar, is this what a dog's ears feel? The jingle of coins in pocket as we race between cars, the sear of horns, someone's overdone dolby dream

Mother No, it's just I haven't been using the phone much. I can't really enjoy it because the ear
No, there's nothing really wrong with it, just a little wax
Well, all right, it's actually a bigger problem
No, I have a good doctor
Yes, I'll take the name of this other doctor
I really have to go
I really have to go
What did you say?
No, that's not a sign of how bad it is

Northern trees So much more quiet up here in the mountains. No, I had no idea you were calling me

Nostalgia You're drooling after skirts while I sit in this ringing place, you're lamenting the end of rock because I can't handle the car radio?

Old poet Oh the overwhelming despair of it all. I am at the reception by the box wine, I am staring at a woman with too much eyeliner wearing a trenchcoat cinched around her break-able waist. She has decided to kill my heart with her heels, but she is holding her ear shut as she holds up the glass of blood. She says to me after my best lines, What did you just say? I'm sorry, I have this thing—pointing with red-painted dagger fin-ger at her lovely shell of an ear. when she says it no longer works, I want to point to my crotch and agree with her. Oh the viagra of youth, the sedative of social occasions. I'd like to take her home and murmur obscenities in that ear, it would be so safe because she can't hear me

Otitis media with perforation A wail from somewhere, three a.m. Shoot me, says the stoned caterpillar as it sits devouring the mushroom

Patch We can sew it shut like a patch on the knee of your jeans, just need a few months for nature to decide which way she's going to go

Patience Rat under the tracks waiting for the subway train to pass. Weak me, meanwhile, holding my ear shut, thumb against the lobe like a nutcase

Perforation Still there. What? Still there. What? Still there. Oh

Phone Don't call me on the phone, I'm still underwater. I'm busy listening to the blips and clicks of the currents against the reef

Prayer Got water in my ear, waited for death but couldn't hear it calling, so it slunk away like a rejected dog

Q-tip Get that away from me

Rain Rainstorm over a meadow, gunmetal sky shot through by a sudden sun

Red A dot in the egg, the idea is to eat more protein to promote healing, the idea is not to get sick when you see the dot in the egg

Scrapyard Yellow cranes are smashing through the junk, creaking enormously, strife and friction of metal against metal, can we go?

Sentimental A crushed crocus in the snow, a poodle's rheumy eyes, single note from a cello, there are no more single notes

Seagulls Just caught descending through the corner of the elevated subway window on the way to the hospital, the in-

and-out operation. Could be seagulls, could be angels, silent,
blessing

Silence No such thing

Subway Did they just say that was the last stop? And where
are we going now? And why are the lights out? Do you know I
have an appointment? Is that the sun?

White Soft rustle of the lab coat at my face, the doc is blue
eyes fringed with the lashes of compassion, of excellent training, says you will be fine, and I say but I can't really hear you
and he says but you just did

You Your lips are shells from the farthest corners of the cabinet, biological wonders, specimens, mirror lovers, I miss your
voice

THREE SISTERS

It was a great big family that lived in a great big house and some littler houses, converted from barns and garages, in a thriving upper-middle-class town in New England. Three sisters bought the place back in the early '70s with money from their parents, Midwestern Jews. The sisters wanted to escape any trappings of being trapped and to define life for themselves. Their marriages, in various states of undoing or beginning, came with them.

It was a house of some chaos but much love—fervent, eye-opening, heartbeating love—watching each other's kids play and grow, thinking they created a new way of life that the children would take for themselves, having been shown that the world, with its nuclear families and two-car garages and three squares a day, could turn on you in horrible ways.

At this house you could make a giant pot of chili and leave it on the spindly-legged stove for the kids to eat all day. You could leave your son with your sister and go protest the war.

You could share shampoos. Share stories, over and over, until they were stitched into quilts to keep you warm all night. None of the sisters were particularly good cooks or seamstresses or housekeepers, but they kept their families warm with these stories. And others—friends, loves, husbands—shared the stories too, until they also felt like part of the family. But really, they were not.

When the stories were exhausted, like the one about an old friend's failed marriage to a housepainter-poet (his pile of paint cans still rusted in the basement), the story of how the sisters came to live here was unfolded and laid out.

The oldest sister was first to leave the Midwest. She was a rare musical talent but received not a nod from their parents, who outspokenly preferred she find a husband and get some padding on that stick figure already.

She went to California, as most people looking for life did back then, to breathe the rebellious air and grow her hair and prepare for whatever came next. She met a scientific genius with impressively dark eyebrows. Together, she in a flowing caftan with a suitcase of sheet music, he in a corduroy jacket with elbow patches, they moved to this New England town, where he got a job teaching his esoteric approach to science that few understood. He had some tendencies, like uncontrollable rages. But they lived in a little house down a hill and had two children, a boy, a girl, and he mostly kept himself in check.

The middle sister was next. She had a voice of steel wrapped in gauze, strong at the core, breathy on the outside, a voice that held light, and a head for lyrics no one else remembered. She took up with a political scientist who was the darling of his mother, a disturbed woman who trained him to be invisible, to only come to life deep inside his head, to otherwise just bring her teacups of lapsang souchong and celadon saucers of tranquilizers, and occasionally retrieve her from the sanitarium if his father was off at a nightclub making deals. That sister and the political scientist moved, of course, to California, where he got a teaching position and wore a corduroy jacket with requisite patches. But they soon had a dispute over the color red, which she wore in an effort to feel less untouched, but which scared the bejesus out of him in a way that had no rational explanation. And so he went deep inside himself and didn't come out, and the middle sister took their son and escaped, following a long, circuitous route to a bluegrass troubadour in Ohio.

At this point the youngest sister had dated a few men who found her high voice and swift humor adorable, but were befuddled by her occasional displays of will. Then she met a tall man with mixed aspirations and a matinee-idol face, or it would be if the features were straightened out, as she said, but anyway he's handsome enough for me. They married. Had a son.

Back in Ohio among the bluegrass the middle sister's son got older. He saw himself facing a future of violent hicks in junior high, who already threw stones at him for being different, who called him fatso and threw stones for that. He'd pass the junior high building with his only friend and shudder. One day he announced to his mother that he could not go there because if he did, he would die.

Then what do you want to do? she asked him in all seriousness, for she always took him seriously, unlike how her parents discounted her.

He said, I want to go to New England and live with my aunt.

So she packed him on a bus with a suitcase full of socks and sent him to her older sister's.

He became the ward of his aunt. He played with her children, the son who was also possibly a genius, if that explained how bizarrely the boy acted. (The boy had a lazy eye he intentionally loosened in its socket to freak out his litter sister, a forlorn girl who created domestic disputes between her dolls that resulted in lost limbs.) One day his aunt's husband lost his job as a star science professor due to an inability to control his rages, and that night, made himself die.

Phone calls—before cells, cordless, conferencing or call waiting, or emailing or internet surfing for the best flight while talking, connected the sisters all night, like Dixie cups on strings. Two inched the other out of her despair and inched themselves, with each call they made, each plan, to her rescue. We're coming, they said.

You don't have to, the older sister lied. I'll be all right.

See you tomorrow, they said.

It took the middle sister fourteen hours and some godawful radio to get there, but she smacked the dashboard of her rickety orange station wagon, daring it to break down, and so it didn't. She had loaded it to the gills—with beer, sweaters, her guitar, her oldest son's collection of empty liquor bottles she hadn't let him take on the bus, her two other sons, who were young enough to wear diapers and threaten each other with the contents. She stopped once, at one a.m., for gas. The youngest sister cut to the chase and booked a redeye flight for herself, her tall husband and their baby—who slept, thankfully, and looked more like his father every minute, but with features rounded in that innocent way.

There was only one thing to do: find a safe place, big enough for everyone to have their own room, for husbands or lovers to have workshops, studies, darkrooms, two bathrooms so the guys didn't have to piss outside. Beyond that, it didn't matter. The sisters knew an inheritance was coming: their parents had been loudly socking it away. They knew how much they'd have to work with, since their parents announced amounts as a matter of pride. But who would have thought that they, with their long hair and dreamy eyes, would be so calculating?

The middle sister called up her father and said, Dad, we have to buy a really big house. Why not just fork it over now? Everything's a mess. You'd be doing us a favor. To her surprise, he did. He said, Just don't tell your mother, then wrote the check.

This sister was already feeling the stirrings of a business-woman, which also surprised her. She said, When we find the right house, we pay cash. We borrow from no one, we owe no one. We'll be safe.

They found a Victorian heap with turrets and overhangs,

built by a prosperous doctor once known for his fast horses and formal garb. The house had fallen on hard times, used by a university to house professors, and occupied most recently by a notorious guru of the psychedelic lifestyle, until he was kicked off the faculty for dosing his students. Love beads still hung from a bathroom hook, which the older children took as a promising sign. They crawled through the house's nooks and crannies, looking for leftover acid. They found mouse carcasses, squirrel's nests, a silver dollar that briefly suggested great mystery. But no stash.

Their mothers did not mind them looking. Didn't even mind when the children decided to sleep in the living room, heaped like puppies. As the children grew up, any rules they had were ones they constructed: No one, including Mom, enters my room without the password. Tuesdays I eat apples, nothing else. Since I never get sick, I get to play pretend-sick because I hate my teacher and need a break from school. And: Grownups can't tell me what to do until they stop making so much noise on school nights, which they will never do, so that's that.

To themselves the sisters thought, genetics is stronger than we expected. Each child was sharp, willful, good with money. Still, the sisters shielded them from the suffocating dotage of the grandparents, who forever tried to dress up the girl and cut the boys' hair, and told the sisters that if they just abandoned their messy, unconventional life in that drafty house already, and just came home to get decent apartments in a nearby high-rise, all would be forgiven.

The children grew up. More were born. The sisters lost and gained husbands, renewed marriages, and no one moved far away except for that oldest son—who had sparked the entire arrangement in the first place by refusing to be stoned by smalltown hicks. He went to live on a school bus back in the same hayseed territory that once terrified him, then sought his fortune as a musician, renting a New York hovel and touring the world in vintage suits. Of the rest, the girl became a librarian. Some of the boys became outstanding carpenters, helping various husbands who were handy, and some who were not, fix up the property and renovate the garage, the barn, the attic. Within twenty years the place was sparkling and populated, although the Volvo-owning neighbors shook their heads at this whole communal thing, wondering if it would drive down the value of their houses (it did not).

The grandparents had been restless strivers, the first generation in a new world. They held onto their dreams of being rich, being seen, having conveniences, having a maid. In their world the women wore diamonds and got their hair done on Fridays, and the men wore pinky rings, had a good cigar over cards. Then the sisters threw off the conventions of marriage whatever the cost, and found themselves, then found better mates, and had children while holding fast to ideals of personal freedom and independence.

But the children: what could they hold onto, besides a giant house? What did they have to work against? Nightly, they drank beer with various girlfriends and boyfriends, eating toast and jam and making French fries in the oven. Buddies came over and said it must be amazing to live in a mansion with four-teen-foot doors and giant fireplaces, to always have so much food around, even at three a.m. after watching a slew of movies. How great to have that many cars in the driveway to borrow, to go get ice cream at Store 24 anytime you got the urge.

The children had plans for the future, but for now it was nice to stay put. Gradually, the daughter found a husband. The sons found wives.

From here, everything changes for a while. The story becomes about the middle sister, and the three wives of her three sons. Maybe it was coincidence that the three wives had things in common, like brown hair grazing their shoulders. They all stood between 5'6" and 5'8", weighed nearly the same. Their names fell midway down the alphabet in neighboring letters: two were named Kim, one Liz. Each loved her husband deeply, having done enough living to know the difference between a good man and a not-so-good man.

On this, all bonded with their mother-in-law, separately from being her daughters-in-law. But that made things kind of messy. For a mother's first allegiance is always to her child. And this is where the story starts.

RUBBER DAYS

Floating on a bed in this all-white room, kept company by the buzz and tick, the monitors, the systems array. I am a head case. A pale girl with limp hair and a skullcap made of gauze and plaster. A new look.

This by way of my introduction is not self-pity, because I'm just delirious, really, that's the prize in my Cracker Jack. The prize in my Cracker Jack? I was cracked by a Jack.

My name is Vanessa. I came from Ohio, from a mother's empty house in a wintry field. It's all a northern, unheated blur now: our scrabbly yard and Lake Erie smell, perch on Fridays at the All U Can Eat, snow-frozen feet in wet sneakers, old rusty car coughing itself awake, midnight sky turned white by the cold, prairie wind rumbling my girl room, rocking the dresser free of my hairbrush, my glass horse figurines. I'd lay sweaters on the floor to catch their nightly fall. Mornings, my mother would watch me gather up the fallen.

You'll go places, she'd say.

And so I did.

Say more, says the blue-shirted reporter guy who's in the orange chair a mile across the room.

I'm twenty-eight. At twenty-eight you're still supposed to feel omnipotent. Like you'll live forever.

That so? he says. Can you be more specific?

No, I tell him. Hardware's a little fried. And my story comes out the way it wants to.

He says, Oh. No, it's not Friday.

I used to say I knew where I was going. I left my mother's gray house, left the stand of cottonwoods and the old porch swing and headed south to escape the winter and start a whole new life. First year, I thought, I'll get my feet on the ground, find a job, a place, get some friends. Do it slow. A few months in, buy a car. I bought a ticket for a seat on the autotrain. I flew low along the southernbound tracks into a new life. By the time I landed, I was ready to hit the ground running. Screw caution, I thought, awed by the happily blinding sun. Whatever comes my way, I'll take it.

Now they say, *Try to remember*. My head's a tumbling clothes dryer, set on endless high heat.

Apparently I know something they need to know. Or they think I know it, though I honestly don't know that I do.

Try to remember, the reporter guy says.

There are reporters and a detective and nurses and doctors, and then there are miscellaneous. Some people I can say some things to. Others, I can't.

You authorized? I ask him. Officially?

It was a surprise, he says. And yes, it was awful. You were taken by awful surprise, yes.

The door swings open and I shut my eyes, listen to the bodies moving. I want to see my friends, my lovers, but I'm off-limits to anyone nonauthorized and nonofficial. For how long, I wonder, but there is really no such thing as long or short. How long have I been here? They've changed the dressing four times. And now reporter guy's being replaced with police lady. They do their we're both official do-si-do. Police lady has been here twice. They time her session to the morphine drip, pull back on the dosage when she's here so I can lighten up and think a bit.

They keep talking about someone's welfare. The word does not quite get through the walls of my head, it kind of clangs on the metal, falls flat.

It's all so incredibly heavy. I know that. So incredibly life and death. The thing is this: somebody tried to kill me. And it didn't quite work, and they make a lot of that. I escaped death. If he'd been a little stronger, they say, or if I'd been standing a foot to the left— they make a lot of that too. If he'd had better aim, they say, very good chance you'd be dead. If you hadn't been knocked out, if he'd swung again, if it was raining or the sky was falling or a fire had been lit or a hurricane had actually touched down like it was supposed to, or if my coworker, darling redheaded Lila, hadn't decided to do an afterhours session for one of her neediest, if she hadn't decided to borrow my spurs, if she hadn't decided to check if I was taking a nap on the leather shrink's couch, if she hadn't swung open the door with a great big Lila smile and hadn't found me—

But she did. Lila is not a creature who dwells in the land of If, I have come to conclude from my place in this white room. There is a God or at least a guardian angel and she is Lila and I hope I see her again.

When found, I was apparently unconscious, blood trickling from the top of my head. I was wearing my rubber merry widow and killer stilettos, and I wasn't on the shrink's couch. I was tied to the Jacob's Cross, one of the dungeon devices we had at the house. I was tied to make it look like maybe I was involved in some kind of reverse scene. And of course they made a lot of that, the tied-up part. Really, this whole civilization was schooled on *Gulliver's Travels*, on cowboys and indians, and we all love to think about being tied up, secretly.

Nurse pads in softly and checks the plastic lines. She taps, squints at the drops crawling down their pristine little highways. I love it when they tap.

I backed her off, she says to the police lady. Give it a few minutes and you're good to go.

Police lady has placed the orange chair by the bed and placed herself in it. She looks maybe Cuban, very plucked eyebrows on a fierce at-the-firing-range kind of face, brown hair drawn back, moon forehead shot with frown lines. She sits waiting for my head to clear. Are you ready? she asks. When she asks questions, the eyebrows go up. When I answer, the frown lines come out.

We left off at the flash, she says. Yesterday?

I remember a tiny flash just before it happened.

As it happened?

No, before.

Can we get back to the costume?

Costume?

That you were wearing.

That's my uniform. I was at work. I think I told you that.

At work? You were tied up. You were left for dead. That's your work?

That's not the work part.

Getting nowhere. Want to sit up?

Nurse appears, pulls me up by my armpits. I smell bad floral scent. I'm a rag doll. Police lady frowns and waves the nurse away. She taps her pen on the chair arm: Wake up.

I try. I blink.

Let's work it backwards now, Vanessa. Try that.

Backwards.

You were found in a house of prostitution.

Actually, we don't call it that.

Well, sex is sex, violent or not.

We don't have sex.

Violent sex.

It's not violent.

Can we stay on point here? Working backwards, right? Who do you think did this? Do you remember a face? Features? Hair color, eyes? Anything distinguishing?

I remember faces all the time, but not from that night.

And they pay to beat up girls?

No, I start to say.

She's got it all wrong. I hold up a hand. This world assumes we're the losers in the power game, us poor wretched females. Even the females assume that. The reputedly fairer sex. But I guess I was, right? I am my own worst example. Still, I have to try.

The House was a matriarchy, I say.

House?

My workplace.

It certainly wasn't a church.

She's wrong, but I'll get to that. I try to explain as my neck starts to feel kind of frozen, cables stiffening. It happens when I sit up—something about fibers, frayed and broken. I swallow, try to ease my head loose. Try to explain that usually I do the tying up. That usually there's no baseball bat. There's never a baseball bat. Baseball bats are so not part of the program. There's no siren light. There's just a switch, a whip, whatever's called for in terms of dark and shiny props. But something apparently went terribly wrong that night. Someone broke in.

Police lady taps the pen on her knee.

We think vendetta, she says. Step on anyone's toes lately?

All the time. I mean, as requested. It's called shoe work.

Shoe work.

I nod my head as she takes that in. The head mechanism needs oil.

More what we're thinking is you crossed someone. That's what we think. I'd like a list of all the people you may have crossed.

There is a certain part of what she says that's on her list, her script, then there are the other parts.

I tell her, I can't do that. I can't remember. I try to say, are you sure you mean cross? Because I was found on one, and it makes it just a little confusing to try to imagine. It crosses back and forth in my mind, the context.

She looks at me and the corners of her mouth flex and twitch. She's not getting what she needs.

We'll get back to that, she says.

Look, I say. It's not my calling. Only my job. I kind of lucked into it. I just needed work. I'm not one of those natural-borns.

Maybe one of your clients felt, possibly, a need to fight back?

That's your theory?

Police lady taps that pen again.

Let's try tomorrow, she says, as a vein on my temple begins to test out a ponderous beat. She gives me that look again, the certain twitch, and slips out the door. In her place the nurse comes to restore the dosage. Yes, please, thanks, fine. Questions hurt. One cc of morphine per question would be about right, if I had my way.

Nurse says, Once the skull knits, you'll be good as new.

Just got to do my knitting then, I try to joke with her, cracking a smile I can feel disorganizing my facial muscles. But she just looks at me with a strange kind of concern. Like, look what you got yourself into.

They all have some kind of concerned look. The doctors gather around the bed and flash a kind of bedside, hands-in-the-labcoat-pockets kind of concern. They shake their head. They grasp my hand. It's so sad, they say. You were only down here nine months.

I still am, right? Down here?

This is a County General. Dade, I think, though I can't quite make out the words on the back of my gown, since I can't reach the back of my gown, can't twist to find it, can't reach for it, et cetera. Or it may be some county just above it. They do that, move the victims away from the vicinity, I heard one nurse say. I have no insurance but all fees are being covered by an anonymous donor. I have my suspicions about who it is. So do they. The police lady told me if they find out who the donor is, they probably have their man. *Their* man. I made a pondering face at her, or what I thought was a pondering face. For all I know I was drooling crosseyed. But I think it got through to her.

Guilt, she said, tapping her head. That's why you get a free ride now.

Wait, I tell the night nurse. Don't forget to sign the guest-book. Everyone has to sign the guestbook.

I motion at the clipboard, which sends a searing rip through my inner back, followed by that cold, wet feeling under my skull, ice water running down my neck.

Don't move, she says, wincing for me.

As she works, turning me, snapping on latex gloves to check the bandaging, she does the idle bedside conversation thing.

When did you move down here, anyway? she asks in a melodic, singy voice.

Nine months, and what I gave birth to is a situation. Is a near death. Is two people I love too much. Is who knows. It could be worse, I could be dead. Isn't that what you're supposed to think? Some of this I can hear myself saying out loud, some not.

You want water from the sink? the night nurse says. There's a pitcher here. On your chart it says one glass at a time, max. Your systems are depressed, she says.

I know that.

It's the clotting agent, and the drip. We need to watch the levels.

You think you could kind of lower the dosage?

Well, she says in that children's storybook hour voice. I think you might not be so comfortable then. And then she continues.

And did you drive down here? From the—

Midwest.

Lots of gals come here from the Midwest. The prairie states. I hear it's terribly cold up there. So you drove?

I took a train.

Took a long time?

A train. The autotrain.

No, but it took a while?

When she says while, there's a palpable "h."

Oh. Six days, actually. I was on a train with a whole lot of old people.

That must've been nice, she says, paying attention to how she cuts the sweet white tape running across my brow. She taps it on lightly. Nerves in my backbone tingle happily.

On the train it was a beautiful party. They all passed around prunes and sandwiches and thermos cups of coffee, and we all watched out the window for orange groves, palm trees, racehorses, alligators. First time? they'd ask with their old, wet eyes. Only time, I'd answer. I'm never going back. I'm coming to seek my fortune.

Ah, the nurse says. Fortune.

I'd just turned twenty-seven. That was nine months ago. Must mean something.

You're fastening on to numbers. I would too.

She shimmers before me. I taste copper, vanilla, wheat paste, but there's nothing in my mouth.

Maybe don't try to talk anymore.

She checks my arm shunt with those featherlight gloved fingers. Touch me more, I want to say.

Her hands busy themselves on my armature, my lines, my shunts and valves, my dressings, my levels. When she can, she picks up the conversation again. I'm so soothed by her, I don't want to talk. But I need the company so I try to rally.

And you made a whole new life down here? I bet you miss your friends.

Yes.

She's pulling some kind of plastic sleeves onto my calves, but they're miles away. I can't answer, so I think the answers. Yes. I do miss my friends, my nutso friends, my rag-doll friends, my latex friends. Because it's a criminal case, they told me, no one knows where I am. But I need them, I tried to say. I'm all alone.

I know it's night because you come in, I say to the nurse, and I know by her startled look that I've garbled the words. She gives a short smile, a flat smile. It's all about smiling when you're a nurse, I've noticed, but you don't actually have to rev the motor. It can be an idle, gasless smile. I must have said something kind of obscene, I guess.

Don't hate me, I call as she walks out the door.

I had a client that told me he'd said that to his wife, after he came clean about what he did every Wednesday at three. She said to him, I'm sorry. I can't help it. She packed her bags. He came back to the House. Can I be your houseboy? he said through sobs. I'm free now. I'll carry the sponge in my teeth, I'll lick the mop clean.

Excuse me? the nurse says.

She's come back. She doesn't hate me. Waves of relief.

I'm in your hands. I love you.

She plumps the pillow around my head, which sounds like a dive into churning surf.

We'll need more blood soon, she says, checking the silver wisp of a watch she wears on her capable forearm. She taps at the IV. You're a talker, she says. That's what I'd call you. But feel free.

I was called. I am called. I'm called V by friends, Banesh by my lover, Please Mistress by the men, Excuse Me by the nurses, How's the Patient by the doctors. Before I was pale and concussed I remember feeling dark and sharp, adjusting to the glare of this party town by dropping twenty bucks on a pair of Ray-Ban copies, fazed by nothing, ready to roll. I had a mercenary's optimism. I believed I was invincible. I would make a heap of money and send it home to Mom and make another heap and just bask. I would buy an old car and tool through the hot nights, feeling like part of something.

Door swings open, a melody of two notes. Bloodtaker now, since it's deep in the night.

I remember that's what I believed, I try to tell him. His face is a sad clown, skin ebony dark, lips red. Emmet? I want to say. Is your name Emmet? Wasn't there a clown named Emmet? Emmet Kelly?

Sure, he says, glancing at the nurse. Of course I can raise the bed.

The tray table has not been moved. It sits near the bed but it's too far away for me to reach. So I stare. The crotches of its wheel brackets have great big balls. The liquids sit on the tray, colorful in their containers, rejected, tinfoil tops half ripped off. Bug juice magenta. Something bright green. One was a vitamin drink, one an oral drug. I'll take the oral, I said, and managed half. Please be patient, I wanted to say, but the commissary lady in the blue smock was gone already. I said it anyway. But this room is all about being patient. Is too patient, I think. Steadily ticking and buzzing, like a dog that knows if it waits long enough, it'll get the bone.

When no one comes in for hours I wonder if they think I was mixed up in some kind of evil, godless trickery, that I got what was coming to me, by god, that at the very least I should feel chastised and avoided, at the very most I should—

This morning light sneaks through the blinds, tries to make itself known in the constant fluorescent pool of my room. And this morning the man in black makes the rounds up and down the hall, Minister so-and-so, who supposedly donates his time. He comes in to take my hand and pray for my recovery. It's my turn to mishear. Let us pray for her covering, I hear, and as he mutters quietly I think of a man I once wrapped in gauze from head to toe. A client. Suffocate me, he said. Wrap my nostrils closed. Just for a minute. I sat there watching him for signs of distress. A minute stretched into a tricky hour. I couldn't breathe either. I watched his chest rise and fall, watched him shudder, jumped up when I thought he was struggling, sat back down when he relaxed. I was a wreck afterwards. He just wanted to do it again. He said, I feel like a newborn. He glowed.

Would you like to pray? Minister says. His hair is swept back in a DA, like a country singer. His skin has a grayish, detoxed look.

I fell into a burning ring of fire, I sing to him.

He smiles. Let's just pray, he says in a ministerial voice, pronouncing and then mini-pausing on every word.

Do you know who you look like?

No.

Mr. Cash.

Beg your pardon?

Mr. Johnny Cash.

Johnny Cash?

John, Jonathan, Juan, Johnson, Cash. You don't know? How can you be a minister and not know about Johnny Cash? The angel wrestling with the dark and the light.

I did not say I did not know him. But I am sure I do not resemble him, the minister says.

Your suit. It's a Johnny Cash suit. Would love to borrow it sometimes, if you know what I mean.

And I wink. He blanches, imagining, I hope, a she-devil in black, swinging a devil whip. I'm learning. If you can't join them—

Opening a book for me, Minister? Did you know my father was Lutheran?

I'm stuttering and high. My father wasn't Lutheran. My father wasn't anything at all. Which of course was a problem for my mother.

Got that IV drip firing up all the pistons now.

You should quiet down. You're in turmoil and agitation. I can help with that.

Hey, Minister. I used to say that too. We're two service professionals here, right? I mean, *I* know that *you* know that *I* know. Right? There's sin and redemption. There's heaven and hell. Tension and release. The truth shall set you free. And she lay down on that Jacob's Cross and she saw the light, and the light was white—

And somewhere there is a face, I thought to myself, but all

I see is the edge of a hairline, the top of a brow—

Nice job you did on the minister, police lady the second says.
She's in a beige suit and came in with a shiny metal clipboard,
a cup of black coffee, and a clicka-clicka ballpoint pen. I'm feeling dangerously articulate, so she's come at the right time.

She taps her glasses when she formulates. It's endearing.
She has a slender torso but thickish legs, which she's tried to
hide in white pantyhose. Whitebread blond hair cut across her
wide round face in long bangs, as if she's trying to hide the
red blotches. She's probably sun sensitive and wishes much she
weren't. But the bangs. Big, big mistake. I like her even more
for this.

So, she says. My turn, all right?

Are you up to date?

Not sure.

She wrinkles her nose. I wonder if she's Swedish,
Scandinavian, Irish, something very un-South Florida. She has
an air of awkward flesh wrapped around a core of impeccable
inner cool. I'm loving my mind today, it's freer. Dosage adjust-
ments.

I'm not up on who brought you here, she says. You've told
us a few different things.

A few different people, I guess, I say. I'm hilarious, I'm
golden.

She purses her lips. Sips from the immaculate white cup of
black coffee. I can't seem to go in a straight line with you, she
says.

She's worn a terrible lipstick: tangerine. Another misguided attempt at sunbelt fashion. It leaves a terribly unhealthy wax smudge on the cup.

I can't tell if you have amnesia, or you're out of it from medication, or if you just don't want to tell me or anybody else the truth.

It's just a little gooey, I say, pointing to my head.

Vanessa. What are you, English? Scottish? Do I see pale skin and blue eyes and bonny-black hair?

German descent, actually, on my father's side. On my mother's, just American. The pale skin is because I don't like the sun. It makes me break out. And I dyed my hair black, actually, after the woman who got me into this kind of work. It's really just brown. Greasy, diner-gravy brown. Meatloaf brown. Blue eyes, I don't know where they come from. Milkman maybe.

She doesn't say anything.

I mean, they should probably be red, people around here seem to think.

This line of work, she says, moving on. Clicka-clicka up and down with the point of that pen. A somehow very judgmental look at me propped up in bed.

I'm not a prostitute, I say, and we start all over again.

Nine months ago, a brilliant, December Saturday, I arrived. Stepped off the autotrain and onto blacktop rippling with heat, sky blanched white, all the parked cars glowing in the blazing sun. First impression upon entering the atmosphere of Planet Florida was that it was impossible to move. A sludge of humidity resisted every step. Someone planned this, I thought: the god of leisure. What better way to slow us down? Taxis idled, waiting. I collapsed into one, into an interior heat just like the exterior heat, only the black vinyl seat added an extra sharp bite. Fresh cigarette stink layered over stale cigarette stink. Driver had silver bristles sticking out from his red neck, wore an undershirt, took me to a strip of motels, never looked at me, or to the side, or in the mirror. Just straight ahead at the heat-rippled, empty road.

Shelter. I found a motel with a blue fish leaping out of its revolving sign. Its kidney-shaped pool had a tiled scene of porpoises frolicking along the bottom. I took a room on the top floor, where the sounds of the highway could pass for waves.

The room was on the end, so no one walked past my window. The walkway was lined with astroturf, a sun-blasted ex-green. The railing collided with the rattling fronds of a coconut palm. That night I stood on the walkway and watched the parking lot below. Powerful, fancyish cars motored in and out, doing their Saturday night thing. A little automotive pomp and show. White Camaros, a red El Camino, a baby-blue Cadillac Seville—the old kind, from about 1973, with a white landau roof. For the first time I knew who they'd made those cars for, all those two-tones and overwrought and extra-long and white seats and burled-oak plastic veneer: people in Florida. For pimps, and for people in Florida. Motors revving as they pulled out, squealed around the corner, headed left and then right onto the highway. Heading for danger. For life and blood and hot-climate types of encounters, or at least the potential for them.

For a week I stayed in, watching the Spanish channel. Ate at the Howard Johnson's right next door. Tried to eat aquatically, as if to acclimatize: clam chowder, fish and chips, fried clams, fish chowder. It all tasted the same, like old grease, a slightly alcoholic tinge to the tartar sauce, but one meal including French fries would last all day. Got used to heat boring into the top of my head, my feet.

Then I ventured farther. Walked down the road until the noon sun was too much, and then ducked into a dark-looking bar with a help wanted sign in the window. I'm an open book, I thought, let the wind find the right page. And why not? I decided. I would bartend.

Inside, in the beer-scented, amber light, were three people. A bartender leaning on the counter, polishing something. An old man passed out at a table in the corner, underneath the tacked-up life preserver. A girl at the other end of the bar. She watched me sit down at the counter with the application.

Shit, she said, walking over. I walk in here for the first time and wonder why, and here you are.

She spoke like half big sister, half con artist. She flicked her ashes on my application and said, Screw that, all right? She clicked her gum Spanishly. She had black hair razzed into a spiky pageboy, china-red fingernails, her cigarette was black with gold trim. She wore an open Hawaiian shirt over a red bikini top, a red skirt, red high heels. Looked tremendous and fierce and very unbeachlike.

She said, Why don't you try something real?

Are you a beer ad? I said back. I'm a girl, see?

You mistake me, she said. I'm your ticket. I'm leaving town and I was looking for someone to take over my life. I'm sick of everyone. But my life here, it's been something else. Someone should have it, but no one I know deserves it.

That could be good or bad, I said. I thought she must be high. Or she's just crazy and doesn't know it. She was acting like a narrator in a high school play. She took a theatrical drag of that elegant cigarette. I looked down at the application. It said, PRINT NAME. For some reason I felt like arguing with that particular instruction.

Hey, the girl said. Truly. I want to give it to a stranger. Cash. Power. If you don't take it, then what are you going to do?

I'm not a big one on plans, I said.

And I'm right you don't even have a car? I saw you from the window walking down the road.

Don't need one, I lied.

Sure, she said. And you live in a motel but you're from where, exactly?

Ohio, exactly.

I thought, Fine, I'll talk to her. She's not going away. I have encountered my first native freak.

Ohio, she said. The heartland. Well you've escaped that, anyway, at least the heart part. And you flew?

Took the autotrain.

She raised an eyebrow.

It was all I could get.

Apple's going to have to fall a bit farther from the tree to stay fresh in this type of sun, she said, stubbing out one, lighting up another.

What?

Ever dye your hair?

Red streaks, last year.

Got muscles? Like this?

She flexed her arm. Touch, she said.

I did. Something in her voice. And underneath a stretch of white velvet skin was a ball of iron.

Occupational, she said. Now you.

Just two girls in a bar comparing arm muscles. The bartender was still polishing, hadn't even looked up. She cupped my bicep in a cool hand and I felt a jolt.

You're wiry, she said. That's good.

For what?

Want to make enough cash to buy a house? Want to make enough to buy a 1957 Bel Air as cherry as a maraschino?

She hoisted a red duffle bag and plopped it on the table.

Take it, she said. I've done my time, now it's back to Pittsburgh before my skin burns right off. She started writing phone numbers on a napkin. The top one, just call and then go there, she said. You can take my old room. They're all slackers but they're sweet. The middle number, he's a friend, kind of, but if you take him to the party New Year's Eve, you'll make a grand.

I won't do sex, I said.

Wait, she said. Just listen. He'll explain. The bottom one, that's for steady work. You'll have to interview. But I can tell you could do it. You're probably a shy little thing but you look a lot braver than that.

I won't do sex, I said again.

There's no sex. It's not about sex. How incredibly ordinary and two-dimensional you think. Be independent-minded. It works better. It keeps you out of trouble, most of the time.

She lit one of those divine little sticks for me and I tasted pepper and licorice on the paper, and a rich tobacco drag after that. From down the other end of the bar slid a glass: a greyhound, vodka and grapefruit juice, which she called the national drink. The fruits, she said. She unzipped the bag for me. Out of its toothy smile glinted up a battery of buckles and straps, shiny patent leather, chrome.

This would not have anything to do with bartending, I said. I sipped slowly—I can't hold my liquor, but that's my secret.

Listen, she said. This is a gift. You're practically on the other side of the equator and this is a frontier town. So flip those little rules upside down and be open-minded and revel in your little muscular self and you'll do fine. And never let any of them get inside you.

I *said*, I said.

No. I don't mean the screwy-screwy. I mean in a bigger way. Just don't.

I took another drink and thought about that. She was looking through the duffle, silently checking things off to herself. She tilted her head, peering in.

What's your name anyway? I said.

She frowned. Names are so boring, she said. Just call me Miss Exit. That pretty much sums me up. I'm finished with this place, and I think it's finished with me. So. She pursed her lips, kissed her fingertip, and touched me on the forehead with it. I felt heat in that tiny place.

I dub you my heiress, she said. You're it.

Back in my motel room I dumped the duffel bag in the corner and took stock of my new life:

- single bed with a mustard-colored blanket of entirely synthetic material that will never soften.
- carpet of indiscriminate dirt color and ashy smell.
- dirty window, right next to the door, with heavy brown tweed curtains on a frozen sliding rail, kept open with a safety pin.
- sun glaring so hard off the auto tops in the parking lot that it bounces through the window and ricochets off my wall when the cars move.
- brown dresser with a field of dead moths and a Bible in the top drawer, inscribed, with a phone number: S Rodriguez, 305/747-5522.
- book of matches in the second drawer from the World Famous Riff-Raff Klub, Fort Lauderdale.
- television with clotheshanger antenna, capable of receiving two stations: Telemundo and, sometimes, the station that

shows *Miami Vice*.
- calendar tacked on the bathroom door, almost done: 1986. Someone put a big X on the 15th of December.
- beige-tiled bathroom with beige walls and beige sink, beige shower stall, beige shower curtain stippled with beige mold, rusty curtain rings.
- bathroom guardian, a finger-long resident cockroach, more politely known as a palmetto bug, which to me just reminds me that it would, if sitting on my palm, dominate it completely.

The finger-long resident cockroach likes to hang out above the medicine cabinet, where the light casts a sinister shadow that makes it look even bigger. Its antenna taps the air when I walk in, probably sending messages to all the other bugs: The girl's back—watch her feet.

I summoned a wave of courage as I stepped forward and opened the medicine cabinet: empty except for a dead black ant and a nearly empty aspirin bottle. Another gift. Clearly someone had decided the aspirin might come in handy to the next guest passing through this party town. And here I was, the next guest. So I dumped the aspirin and rinsed the bottle out. The screech of the faucet sent the palmetto bug whooshing back behind the cabinet. You can come back out, I called as I shut the door behind me and headed down the walkway, astroturf scratching my bare feet.

The old woman a few rooms down opened the door with a bottle of Dominican rum in her hand. She'd offered me rum the first day I was here. It keeps the hair off your chest, she'd said. But I'd said, No, wait until I'm ready to go out.

I'm ready, I said.

She was in a pink nightgown and pink hairnet and pink slippers. The passionate sounds of a Spanish soap opera littered the room behind her. I held out the aspirin bottle.

So small?

Just want enough to walk on, I said. She was extremely deft in her ability to pour the rum from the big bottle into the little bottle. I've got my skills, she said. It takes dedication.

Can I give you a dollar? I said.

My gift to you, she said. From the welcome wagon.

I had decided to accept any and all gifts that came my way. Seeking one's fortune means you don't refuse handouts. The rum was sweet as chocolate.

I headed to the mall, according to Miss Exit's instructions. Just kept walking along the highway, on the foot-wide path called a sidewalk, across the big intersections, sipping on my little bottle of rum. Walked through the double doors of Dadeland Mall tipsy and sweating and feeling reckless, and headed for the Wild Pair.

I was wearing the clothes I'd arrived from Ohio in, but modified. Brown corduroys hacked into shorts. Old penny loafers with new pennies. Man's undershirt. First time that undershirt has seen the light of day, ever, I was thinking. Everyone else was in matching outfits, girls with hair and nails and tight pants and halter tops all matching, in cherry, salmon pink, lemon, orange, lime. The girl who helped me at the shoe store raised one precisely plucked eyebrow when I pointed out the boots I wanted, and pursed her melon lips as she checked the price.

One eighty, she said. She hit her own leg mid-thigh. Up to here, she said.

Dangerous heel-height and plastic calf-hug and heat building up under the shaft and a whole new feeling up my legs, right up to the fringe of my cutoffs. I took it slow across the suddenly hazardous store carpet. In boots like this, you walk knees first. Strutted slow past the racks of jewelled sandals and dyable pumps, caught a glimpse in the mirror. As far as the boots stretched I looked like Wonder Woman's bad little sister. Or Emma Peel. Or Catwoman. All those tightly packaged power girls. Above, like a skinny mechanic.

I thought I'd wear the boots out until I tripped on the shiny tile by the hiking boot display, nearly went over, thought better of it. I'll keep the box, I said, as if nothing had happened.

At a clubwear boutique called Scandal I bought a black rubber dress with a keyhole neckline. It smelled like a bicycle tire. At the keyhole there was supposed to be cleavage showing. On me there was just a pale, bony plain. But still, it clung, almost gave me ass and hips.

Miss Exit had said, If you have bucks left over, do your hair. Do a China Doll, I told the stylist at the Wave and Trim. Do it black. She did my nails blood-red to match. Don't go out in the sun too much, she said, or the hair'll fade.

You are a fantasy, Miss Exit had instructed. Just a really tough one.

In the motel I felt different, like *Guess what I did*. I hung the new dress on the one rusty hanger provided in the closet, really just a recess in the wall next to the bathroom door. A little red spider jumped on, waved a leg as if to check it out, jumped off, like, This is not part of any natural world *I* know. And still full of aspirin-bottle rum, this fascinated me. Which in itself fascinated me until I dropped down, rung by rung, to the obvious conclusion: I was spending too much time alone. Inside. A mole fascinated by a speck of dirt.

I went outside into the sunblast to go swimming in cutoffs and t-shirt, but got dirty looks from the couple basking in the dirty chairs. Close up, the pool was littered with debris: leaves, paper cups, bugs, berries, red flowers rotting to black, a whole flotsam-jetsam thing gathering at the steps. Fine, I thought. I skimmed the water with my toe and felt sufficiently wet then to just sit in the sun, wear my new sunglasses, feel heat on my skin. Opened my eyes and the couple was in the pool, doing some kind of treadwater embrace, belly to belly, flabby leg wrapped around flabby leg.

Ah. Fluids, possibly, releasing in there underneath the vegetation. Sinking to the bottom, settling on the tiles, catching in the grout.

Gave up the swimming idea.

Back in the room, I stared at the generic palm and sunset photo under cracked glass. Straightened the cigarette-burned lampshade on the night-table lamp.

Noticed a thousand insect husks embedded in the carpet: shells of dead roaches, grubs, ant sections.

Went for more rum.

They had bedbugs in this place too, the rum woman said, pouring me a paper cupful. Same kind of cups, I noticed, that were bobbing around the steps in the pool. Dixie, a swarm of daisies in pink and blue.

Bedbugs? I don't feel any bites.

They fumigated. They announced it the morning of the day. Can you imagine? The morning of the same day. I personally saw it as a ploy to get into our rooms and commit theft and larceny. And therefore I didn't want to go. I said I'd rather wear a towel over my nose than have them kick me out of my own room. I have things here. Valuable things. They called my ex-sister-in-law to convince me otherwise.

They had her number?

I was required to provide a next of kin in case of any unforeseen, she said. There are not that many of us. We seem to inherit conditions. And with me, I suppose they might surmise I am mentally off or more likely to croak or something.

You look pretty healthy to me, I lied.

Didn't you have to do that? she wanted to know.

I shook my head. We both took long swigs of our rum. She looked a little troubled that she'd had to do something I didn't have to do. So to be kind I said, I gave them a list of people anyway.

Maybe with you they think there is nothing yet to foresee. Anyway my sister-in-law showed up and convinced me. I still don't know how I feel about that.

The spraying?

My ex-sister in law. It's not right having someone who's not even blood chase you out of your own home.

It wasn't that I was happy. It wasn't that I wasn't. I was just there. I was just inside or outside, here or there. But I expected that. I just went with it. Then, the afternoon of New Year's Eve, the motel was jumping. The room next to mine held a trio of inebriates babbling in Japanese, and we busted open the pass-through door between our rooms and they shared their champagne. I pantomimed getting shit-faced and they cheered. They pantomimed getting shit-faced. But you *are* shit-faced, I yelled at them, and they shrieked with delight. They turned on the television, finding it hilarious. News, a traffic report—all hilarious! They decided to go for a swim. Hilarious! You swim! they yelled.

No! I yelled, and we all cheered.

It was barely sunset, and the weatherman was riffing on our unseasonal heat. I don't know, I don't know, he finally said, throwing up his tan hands. Just get drunk, okay? I went to the ice machine, iced down my skin, pulled on my new dress. At first the rubber felt sleek and cool. At the payphone, I dialed the number. A woman was leaning out her motel room window, watching me. I waved. She made a shooing motion. There was always someone watching. Everyone seemed used to it.

It was heating up inside that dress, inside the brand new thigh-hi boots. An investment, Miss Exit had said. But you'll get the money back. Hadn't even started working and already I was pouring sweat. From the phone I could just reach the ice machine, grab a cube, run it down my skin before it melted in my hand.

Oh it's you, he said.

I heard Southern drawl, boredom, bourbon on the rocks clinking in a glass.

And who are *you*?

I'm just a boy who lives in a messy little bungalow and likes to go out and repent before the crowd. Can't wait to meet you, really. It's a little potluck, you know, this soiree, everyone is bringing something. I'll bring refreshments, you can bring the—

Whip, I said.

And there it was. I stepped into Miss Exit's scary shoes with one word. I've always been so adaptable really, so good at doing the new job, just not the old one.

Well hallelujah, he said. She told me you were good.

There's a bargain a woman makes with the world when she's running away: Don't miss me, because here's this other girl, and she's taking my place, and you'll love her, she's just like me. And then there's the flip side, which is the lie she makes to her replacement: *Here, take my place, anyone can do it.*

But the thing is, I did. It turned out I was good at it. A quiet girl from up north whose nose used to run at the first sign of cold, who got dry skin at her elbows and the corners of her mouth. You could say I warmed up down here in this brash, hot place, and turned into someone else.

And isn't that what we want, when we leave home?

At about seven, when the motel was starting to jump,

he pulled up in a fancy yellow Jeep. He was a gray-templed, stocky young man, and he introduced himself as the wastrel black sheep in a fine old family of sea captains and dowagers. He said he made it a point to lead a pointless life. I am subsidized to within an inch of my ridiculous existence, he slurred as I climbed in the jeep. And my father and his fathers before him were bastard tycoons. He was dressed in a rumpled tux and old-fashioned blue sneakers, had an air of a drunken skipper having a marvelous time. He reeked of whiskey. It's very old, expensive whiskey, he said, passing me the silver flask.

He saw the boots up close now. But never mind me, he said.

Never mind, then, I said.

He waved the flask at the shabby quadrangle of the motel. I hope you don't live here, he said.

Miss Exit had said, make it short, snappy. Be mean, don't be kind. It would have been so nice to be in a conversation, to talk about meeting her, to just relax.

Shut up and drive, I said.

We drove along the subtropical boulevard, steam netted in the heavy air, dripping off the tree canopy above us. He kept saying, So darn hot for January, and I said, It's still December, chafing in my gear. He set us up with pharmaceuticals, a red one for him, a yellow for me. Try it, he said. The last batch of 1986. Can't wait to kiss this year goodbye.

The paper cup was soft as cotton. The water chaser had migrated from inside the cup to pool warmly in my hand. I thought, I'm going to make a grand in one night. I said, What's your name?

What would you like to call me? he said. She had so many names.

An accident, I said, as he veered around a pile of palm fronds in the road, nearly tipping us.

Oh I am, he said, in that upperclass voice. One day, true story, my father looked at my mother, who had been a beauty in her day but by twenty-four looked like a cow, and he felt sorry for her. Or maybe he just says that and really what he felt was scorn. And it turned him on, you know, my father being a bastard, and so here I am. Henry the third. Henry Henry Henry. I've always thought that explained a lot about me, don't you think?

As he asked me that, he was looking straight at me, for a long moment, instead of the road. I grabbed the wheel. Slow the fuck down, I said.

I like your style, he said. You are young but so commanding.

He continued to race along under the trees, popping various substances in his mouth, sharing. I was feeling a specifically exaggerated clarity come on like a new set of glasses, like I knew therefore exactly what I was doing, like every leaf and frond we passed had a preordained pattern, so trippingly clear in the sticky air, and the speed of the jeep started to feel like a good thing. I couldn't look around fast enough.

Doesn't it feel just awful? God is so cruel, Henry Henry Henry said as he passed me a second flask, warm gin to slake my unslakeable thirst, and I wasn't sure if he meant the pills or the weather, since I was pouring sweat under that dress, hadn't yet learned, you see, about talcum powder. He skidded suddenly, I slid nearly all the way off the seat. He said, I am so proud to be bringing such an elegant someone to the Chairman's.

The scrollwork gates whirred open and we snaked towards a fake Spanish sprawl of a house, its giant entrance spotlit. The tires crunched the gravel, the down-here-it's-known-as-chatahoochie, such a swinging name for a bunch of rocks, and Henry Henry Henry steered right at a boy in black shorts and a little party mask, and the sky was turning lavender as the sun set. We climbed out and hit the steambath air and the boy valet shot the car expertly onto the lawn between a silver Mercedes and an orange Ferrari (even stoned I know my cars), and I knew right then that the next day, as dawn broke over the carnage, an entire crew would come to repair the damage, and the lawn would be reborn, rustling vivid and seamless green, and the chatahoochie would be raked into some Zenlike pattern, and whoever was still here would be fed some kind of delicate little rolls and strong coffee, then sent discreetly on their way.

The party's host, the Chairman, was so jaunty and raw-looking, like he existed on a diet of lemons and gin, that I wanted to call him Godfrey. He answered the door dressed only in a tuxedo shirt. An absurdly cheerful red bowtie stood up between the points of his tuxedo collar, and his cock hung down like a mollusk's arm from between the shirttails, and in a prairie drawl coated with new money he beckoned us in the giant door with a *Ha-Happy Nude Year and come on in and come.*

Behind him was the party, a steamy vista of bodies romping in the giant sunken living room. Gliding waiters moved silver trays of champagne above the hundred guests, most of whom were not walking, were at least half naked, white butts and brown legs, brown butts and brown legs, pale banker's butts and hairy banker's legs, and caramel and mahogany and pink and alabaster with random accents of lace and leather, the odd glinting chainmail or blink of a jewel. They were heaped onto each other in piles and sub-piles and couplings and trios, biological shapes heaving in unison and counterpoint. And overlooking them all on a long glass table at the other end of the living room was the centerpiece: a lovely little Christmas tree, barely two feet high. A tannenbaum-ette. For 'twas still the season after all, despite the heat wave.

Look at that, I said to Henry. A deeply tanned woman with palomino-tail hair and flashlight breasts in a black leather skirt sauntered up oozing strawberry scent and stood next to us.

It can't be real, he said.

Of course it's real, she said, in a low rasp far older than her body looked. But *you* wouldn't know real if it hit you on the head. It is bon-zai, she said to me. From Pop Frosty's Gar-den Hut. He is such the wi-zard. He makes Ja-pa-nese bonsai from Japan. An ama-zing place. Everybody knows.

She flared a nostril and caught a drink off a passing tray. Her throat constricted and moved. Well then, she said, motioning back towards the party. She headed into the pile, parting the bodies as she walked through, long pale hair hanging straight and still.

She wanted me, Henry said.

Me on one riverbank and the glass table on the other, a raucous current of flesh and tongues between us. Henry Henry Henry headed for the bar. I telephotoed on the tree, just staring. The little branches were so artfully covered with little drifts of snow, as if a miniature storm had recently fallen from a tiny patch of Alpine sky just above it, and had landed in picturesque symmetry, like some kind of windborne waltz. A lovely little tree perfectly dusted with artificial snow, standing mute over the piling and coupling bodies, the occasional slaps and laughter and the clink of glasses and blurry New Year's toasts. A man said, Resolution? The French resolution! And with that ten people descended upon that tiny live tree with their tiny gold straws, and the snow, I realized, was actually real. Only it was the other kind of snow.

It was that kind of party, to put it stupidly. And I did get stupid, numbed by the yellows and then snowed under until that part right above the back of my throat began to click, so I went for the champagne. Which produced a throb and an ache, and to chase that off I went to find Henry Henry Henry, dug into his jacket for more yellows and chased them down with more champagne, and then the throb migrated to the outer perimeter of my skull to reform as a clamp across my brow. Then suddenly it broke off, and my head disconnected, the capsule breaking away from its mother rocket to explore a deeper part of space. And again I felt clear as a bell, if a bell could ring without making a sound. Just a silent movie of a bell, where you watch it swing in slow motion, and imagine it's going to start making noise at any moment, but you're wrong.

Were you asleep? a nurse says.

I hear the rustle of her pantyhose and feel a little pinch in my arm, and she murmurs, Pinch. But it doesn't hurt at all. And I hold the frame, hold my breath, waiting for the warm crawl of the drip, and there it is. Good, she says, and I smile, I melt. I am still here, maybe it's been a week, maybe two, maybe three, in some sort of guarded room in a state of suspended animation, where they evaluate and test and evaluate again, and then someday perhaps I'll get to leave, or get to stay. The blinds rattle softly over the currents of the piped-in AC. Somewhere in this building there is a central core, like a heart making everything work. They keep it cool in here, which I suspect is for the visitors. They are working, I make them sweat. They say, Try to remember what happened, just try. It's a long story, I try to tell them, but it's like they listen with their eyebrows, and all they hear is empty.

The taste of coke through a gold straw is different than the taste of coke through a hundred-dollar bill, Henry said. Here, try. And then he was waltzing in place by himself, and peeling off clothes, and saying, Well, it's New Year's Eve. I watched him, knowing that this city seizes the day the worst way it can, and tonight everyone was going to act terribly so they could regret it the next day and promise, promise to be better, to not lie or cheat or flirt or misbehave, or at least not drink so much, ever, ever again. And Henry the third, now in underwear and socks and dog collar, begged me, Oh please can't we show them how good I am, please can't we do a little scene? Please, for another two hundred, another four hundred, he whispered. Pretty please with money on top so I can start this year off right?

A holiday bonus: I wasn't boiling dishes in a Hobart anymore. That's what I chose to forget, isn't it? I was resplendently clad and propped up on wicked heels, I was going to be temporarily rich. If anything it would be interesting, I told myself, and so I made Henry wait while I pretended to consider, time all out of proportion from all the chemistry, so maybe it was a long time, maybe not. I made him beg until I said, All right, all right, and they cheered, our sudden audience, now bored with fluids and hoping for something stronger.

They cleared the living room and someone croaked *Speech* as Henry went to his knees and I warmed up my whip arm, swinging slowly, this was interesting, I could do this, feeling the pharmaceuticals buzz down the bone as my blood realigned to better absorb all those bad compounds. I rolled the whip back and forth, pulling air in with both nostrils to clear my head as Henry shivered, waiting. There was a moment when I thought, Stop now, or that's it, it all starts. But I didn't. Instead, with one swing, I joined the sweaty, decadent ranks. I shut my eyes and saw blue sky, white, swollen clouds, and opened them to the pale hillock of a man's white back, the black lash snaking, blank faces, watching. I shot it out, cracked the air, popped it gunpowder loud, the bodies around us sighing and exclaiming, and I was supreme for that second, that awful, turn-the-corner second. Then I realized: I was just the entertainment. I flinched, Henry flinched, though he'd promised to not move, and I got him high across the back, nearly at the neck. He twisted around, looking bewildered, and I pretended to ignore him, getting ready to land another one. If I'd known what I was doing, I remember thinking, I could've snapped it right on his ass, or across the ribs, but I didn't, and there we were, and I thought, Now I'd really better stop.

But he didn't want to stop. I'll remember this always, the dignified suffering in that bloated face. The guests cheering. Through tears he was beaming. For isn't it wonderful to be known for something? He swallowed another pill to dull the pain, his turkey back striped red. I stepped back so the whip wouldn't catch him so high, but it did, he gasped sharply and I wanted to make sure he was all right, but suddenly it was time, the host and everyone surged around us to count the year closed, and a skinny girl threw herself onto the carpet and another girl jumped on top, then that valet boy jumped under a waiter, and each final second of the year was sounded with a smack on someone's ass, 9-8-7-6-5-4-3- until it was Happy 1987, all screams and half-assed versions of "Auld Lang Syne."

I sat dizzy on the sectional as Henry got to his knees, looked blurrily into my eyes and proposed a toast, offered me champagne out of his cupped fat-fingered hands as tears streamed down his face, and for his sake I jammed my boot heel into his naked thigh and dared him to spill the wine as I dipped down to drink it. I could barely stand the taste, the layer of sweat scent over it. Are you all right, I asked him, and he said, So glad I was with you as the year turned over, and at that so did my stomach. Air, I whispered, trying to stand up, and felt the damp bills pressed into my hand. Through the bodies I went, lurched toward a door, out to the back patio where suddenly, it was quiet.

The night was peaceful, just hanging there over us, above the giant framing of screens that protected the patio. And in the middle was the subtropical moon, a big yellow fool's moon, nearly perfectly but not entirely round. The air was lacy with the scent of oversweet flowers. I stood at the edge of the house's blue pool, lit from within and staring up at the world like an open eye.

It's so calm, isn't it, someone said.

I stood there. I wasn't quite up to speech.

Like it's mocking us, don't you think? It was a man's voice, calm, lilting and accented, something dry and bitter in it, a little drunk maybe, a little mad. And it had the hollow sound voices can take on near water.

I made him out as a dark form at the other side of the pool.

I like to spend my time near the deep end, he said, and gave a little laugh.

And I headed to a key lime tree planted on a little mound, since right then I was flying, just not in a very level way, and tried to not tilt towards the water. I sat down in the soft ground. Looked up at the fruit glowing under the moon.

This pool is mocking, he said. Large and well-maintained and expensive, but mocking.

I felt drunk and regretful. Maybe it should be mocking, I said, and let myself travel back for a moment to giant fir trees in the snow, the real northern thing where no party like this could ever happen. I thought, I'm really no good at this already. I can't calculate, I'll be the one that lets them all in.

Nonsense, said the voice. You're good at what you do.

I hadn't said a word.

You like to be clever, don't you? Come to parties to beat the boys up.

He waved on a sensor light, which cast its white beam over him. He was lying on a long chair in a tuxedo. Slicked black hair, a gold wristwatch glinting in the water's blue light. It was refreshing to see someone so fully clothed.

You like to watch, I said. You could get arrested for that.

Perhaps you could do the honors, he said, lifting a ciga-rette.

And maybe it was the champagne, the residue of snow and pharmaceuticals, the unmoving air, but I felt my head have to turn back towards the house or my neck would freeze. Sitting on my little island I looked through the picture window. There was a fat man getting down on his knees. They poured cham-pagne down his throat, his hands flew into the air. Palomino Hair knelt behind him, braced her knee into his back and pulled his head back by the hair, gesturing at the crowd for more champagne.

To each his own, said the man in the chair.

Somewhere behind me, something moved along the ground. The air seemed to be getting heavier. Little gnats entered my ear, tortured me quickly, then left. Inside the fat man doubled over and then reared back up, and the woman waved an empty bottle in the air, showing how much she'd just forced down his throat.

You women are, as a species, capable of so much more than we give you credit for, said El Tux.

The fat man rolled onto his back, his stomach heaving. I shifted position under the tree, leaning onto my other arm, and my hand pressed into the hot mush of a rotting lime.

Maybe you should take his place, I said. But I felt like asking, That little scene I did with Henry Henry Henry, did *that* look good? Did it look real? But it didn't matter, did it, what it looked like to him.

I would love to take his place, he said.

And I had my answer. It can't be that easy, I thought, but maybe it was. Maybe it was all show and nothing else mattered, and that made me a little sad. How can anyone get better at anything that way? How could anyone even care?

I would, he said again, and stopped. He waved his hand weakly. I heard him say something almost under his breath, Dios, pero Dios, I think, and another cigarette was produced, that perennial nightlight. Smoke drifted into the mist hanging above the pool. Really, it was quite beautiful. They're all in this beautiful place, I thought, and they do such ugly things. They.

We.

Tux was getting up. Well, he said, hope we meet again. He came halfway over to me as if he was going to shake my hand. May I get your name? he said. He tilted his fine head toward me slightly, some kind of old-fashioned, courtly gesture, it seemed to me, and my neck seemed to be too frozen in position to tilt it back.

V, I said. At that moment, it was decided. That would be my name down here. It had an *I'm not staying* feeling to it. A quickness. I could live with that. It gave me a little crest of happiness and I thought of getting up to shake hands. I seemed, however, to be a little rocky.

Don't get up, he said. He ran a pinkie finger under his eye. Shall I tell you my name? he said. Before I go back in?

No.

Then he was back inside. I watched him through the window: greeted by the host with open arms, he seemed to skate through the room. Everybody knew him. I considered getting up again, going back to make sure Henry was all right. But my work was done. It was good to be alone. My body was heavy, seemed to have grown roots. I felt a little mechanical, my head stuck to the left, trained on the window.

Inside the house the fat man was back on his knees. He gave a tremendous heave, and another, and liquid poured out of his mouth. It is an awful sight, an open mouth with anything coming back out of it. Palomino Hair stepped away as he collapsed onto the carpet. Their audience backed off, done with this little scene, and milled towards other things. And beyond the gasping, struggling man, I could see that tree again, tiny and perfect on the table. Only now it was free of snow.

And that's when I had another little moment, my last New Year's jolt. Because suddenly that little live tree, standing green and blind on the glass table, looked absolutely lost. It caused a little lurch in me, an unfastening, somewhere mid-gut. But I didn't feel sick. Just like some part of me just fell away, like a chunk of snow getting loose and beginning its roll down the side of a mountain. I felt like I was leaning forward but I wasn't, like I was about to lose my balance and pitch head first. I knew, already, that I never wanted go back inside, never wanted to deal with any of these people again, but then there was something else tugging me back, that stupid streak of beginner's luck that keeps you at the table. I considered walking slowly around the patio, looking for that secret door, letting myself out into an entirely different kind of night. I stood up to say goodbye to that little tree and felt like I was falling, tumbling a great way, rolling and breaking apart as I plunged down toward a valley I couldn't see, but knew, somehow, would be there.

The beginning of my avalanche, which would not truly gain momentum for a good long while. Because instead of leaving, I went back inside.

BELMAR

The house the Fleitmans rent rooms in during the summer is a washy pale green that makes Myra feel sick when the sun hits it in the midafternoons. She can't look at its clapboard sides or her stomach will begin to jump. She has to look down as she comes up the front steps. She lives with her family because she hasn't left yet. But she will.

Today there is a chicken boiling in the kitchen pot and peas graying in a saucepan. There is a loaf of Snyder's Bakery rye out on the table, the Fleitmans' table, which is covered in a yellow oilcloth like the other tables in the eating room. Four families live in their rented summer rooms in this big clapboard house run by Mrs. Shlatt, and each family is to Myra worse than the next. Each one has a different way of asking her questions.

So Myra how do you like Belmar? Mr. Lewis says. Nice young men down here.

Have you met Petey down the street? asks Mrs. Marwitz.

Good you don't have the problems eating, Mr. Marwitz says. You know thin girls, they don't look so great.

Ya got someone? says Mrs. Shlatt.

Her mother and father love Belmar. Salt-aired, windy Belmar. Sometimes sunny Belmar. Boardwalked strip on a shrug of land along the Jersey shore. Every Friday during the summer they load their children into the black Hudson for the drive down to the ocean. Myra sits in the back, still and nineteen, and her brother Neil sits next to her, banging his small back against the seat. He is ten. He says, I was born as the war was ending, right?

In Belmar there are so many things for her mother and father to do. Close enough to Asbury Park for a good time. Close enough to Jersey City to drive back home on Sunday night. Close enough to Brooklyn so Aunt Esther—her mother's sister—and Esther's hardworker husband Uncle Al can come overnight. Belmar with all their friends. Mahjong. From her room Myra can hear the clicking of tiles in the afternoon, her mother's strong voice, a soprano, picking up air and strength as she does well. Squaredancing to the boardwalk band every Wednesday Thursday Friday. Strolling the boardwalk at night. Her mother calls it walking the boards. Any name she hears for something, she uses. It's what we can all have in common, she says to Myra, who refuses to believe this.

Her mother does things Myra knows she will never do. She wears a charm bracelet: *Charlie and Rose*. She wears polka dots. She cinches the belt of her sundress so tight she looks like she was built in stages. The softened drum of her torso pushes against the muslin. The flesh gathers in lips at her waist. On the boardwalk at night Myra walks behind them holding on to Neil's restless, sticky hand and pretends the couple walking arm in arm ahead of her are strangers. The woman who brightens whenever they pass neighbors and acquaintances, and who beams to them with her Aren't I Lucky face is not her mother.

Her father is a nice man. A family man. He loses himself in his thinking about his business. Stationery. His store in Newark is a giant room where Myra used to love to go and watch the dust rain down in the sunlight from the papergoods loft. At Belmar he dozes on the beach in his chair. He talks about current events.

This afternoon at the beach the sun beats down onto Myra's legs and she covers her heated shins with *Modern Art* magazine. She calls Neil over for him to put on his shirt. His chest is brown and he stands arching his back the way boys arch their backs when they have shed their shirts at the ocean, spare stomachs sticking into the wind. Near them gulls hop along the shore, their wings spread to dry. Neil spins around in front of her. His ten-year-old feet tunnel a hole into the sand. He plays with the black strands of his sister's hair. He fluffs the short bangs across her forehead.

You look Chinese, he says to her. You look Egyptian.

I do not, Myra says.

You do, he says. He presses at the corners of her eyes to slant them and Myra sees what's in front of her as a blur. You do, he says, see?

I believe you then, she says. Always, in the middle of the grand scenes that happen in their house back in Jersey City or their rented summer rooms, him caught in the middle like a dervish, an imp, whatever their mother wants to call him, she believes him.

In the years between them there would have been another child, but something happened one summer, an accident. Myra was young, younger than Neil is now. There was wailing from her mother's room. Her father's muted voice. The heavy steps of Mrs. Shlatt come to check on things. Myra remembers the felty back of the oilcloth tacked around the bathroom sink where she hid, listening to her mother crying out, chasing any quiet right out of the house and into the heavy night, where Myra wanted to go too. She hid like she would learn to hide—out of sight, but still in the house. For months after that, she listened to her mother the way she would learn to listen—knowing her mother was hysterical, irrational, the trigger of her vocal grieving set off by the arrival of anyone in the room. But still, her mother had lost something, and that Myra also knew.

Neil, he has learned to get attention in that way their mother believes is the way to get attention. A fuss. A little storm. My little hellion, their mother complains to any grownups around the table. Neil listens and flicks nuts out of their bowl. I cross my fingers over that boy. Neil overturns the bowl with the side of his hand and watches the nuts tumble to the floor. You little mischief maker, come here you. Her hands around his face, adoring the curve of his cheek. My little son, she says to whoever's around. What a handful.

The sun is losing its strength. Myra picks up the magazine. She has a string bag for her magazine, her sketchpad, her charcoals. She reads and sketches. She works on perspective. She slants the sight lines of the beach and the ocean. She makes them meet at that infinite point. People walk in front of her but she ignores them. She leaves them out of her sketch so that it looks like a sketch of an empty, peaceful place. Then, thinking of the drawings she admires, the ones by the Impressionists in places like France and Spain, she adds just the hint of a person, just one, in the corner. But it looks awkward, so she adds a few more.

Neil crouches by her, his head dwarfed by her floppy straw hat, watching. You always draw, he says. Why don't you ever go in the water? Why don't you run around?

There are so many years between us, Myra thinks.

The beach is thinning out. Near them Rose is still lying prone in her polka dots on the sand, Charlie's sitting on a beach chair, stoic and sunburnt, looking into the sand and curling his toes as he discusses something with Mr. Shlatt. That senator, he says, that senator who no one believes but no one will stand up to.

Beyond these two men a whole family is gathered around a heavy woman who's slicing a meatloaf on waxpaper. The beach is always arguments, always food. Myra watches this woman, whose suit is a dark wet sack drying on her great body. She watches this woman whose slicing arm waves extra flesh as she works the knife. A breeze carries the smell of peppery meat and cold onions across the sand. Myra holds her breath and feels like she is about to faint. I am only here by accident, she tells herself, I will not be here forever. She pencils over the perspective lines to make them dark and clear. From the front plane of the sketch all the way to the back, a line stretching for miles.

Myra is going to leave New Jersey. She will go to art school in New York City. She will live in the Village. She has planned this with her friend Louise over coffees at the drugstore. Louise's mother is at least a reasonable person but she too has her problems. I should leave too, Louise says, sipping at the cup. She is a sipper, a nibbler. Myra thinks that might be a sign of things bad at home. Wars over food. She has told Louise about her Aunt Esther and Uncle Al who have to strap their daughter down every meal to get any nutrition down the girl. Louise's eyes opened wide and she nodded solemnly. They have planned that this September they will both move out of their parents' houses on the same night. It will have to be at night. Their leaving will cause scenes and their mothers will scream they are ungrateful. Myra can't wait. She will bring her oil paints and her dungarees and her skirts and her carmine lipstick and she will never have to see her mother again.

Aunt Esther and Uncle Al are coming today. They're probably on their way, arguing in their car as they drive down the hot road. Al is a man who holds two jobs and returns from them bitter and full of bile. They have little time for fun. They just managed to get Al time off to come out, a fact Esther repeated again and again on the phone, as if it were a warning of some kind. This morning Myra's mother leaned across the table as she and Myra were sorting utensils and said, Your father still shaves my legs. It was her way of making sure Myra knows she is not like her sister. Myra does not tell her mother anything.

They come back as the sun goes down and Myra can smell the chicken, now boiled down to a stew, as they come in the front hall. Esther and Al are already there, sitting stiffly at the wrong table in the eating room. The Lewis's table. Al is drinking soda water. Their daughter Barbara is trembling in a high chair. Eat, I work for it, Al tells her. He thumbs a piece of bread between his daughter's pressed-together lips. Myra lets him know that she has seen this by looking straight at them. She is storing up lessons from all of them on how not to be.

Aunt Esther was born with dark circles under her baby eyes and a club foot. She once told Myra how, before they all were married, she would sit in the dance-hall chairs waiting for her sister to dance herself into exhaustion, to come back from the middle of the ballroom flushed and giddy. Myra would love to sketch her, the angles of her, the way she stands with one hip up over the normal leg and one hip down over the short one. The way she has a cane, which Myra, before she really knew was it was for, used to find almost as glamorous as the idea of a woman smoking a man's cigar.

They sit around the table and Myra's father slices up the rye bread from the counter. Myra sets the table as Neil gallops up and down the front hall, the utensils held hostage in his fist. Bring them back here, Myra calls. He ducks in ahead of their mother, who's tying on her apron in the doorway. Well Rose, Al says, your son is still a brat.

You stop, Esther says to him.

Myra watches Neil rubbing the sand out of his crewcut and tries to see signs of how old he will be when he leaves. But she can't. His face is young and it contains no plans.

This morning Neil cracked eggs into Myra's espadrilles. She found her shoes sticky with yolk. The eggwhite flaked off the straw. There was no use getting mad. There was no use telling their mother. It would only make her mother all emotional and the rest of the day more difficult. She took Neil by the arms and looked into his distracted eyes and said, I know you think this was funny.

Is funny, he said.

She wanted to say something. About how she is the only one who sees him as a person. About how he'll find that out as soon as he tries to do anything on his own. About how she will be leaving soon, as soon as the summer is over. But she can't. There is always the chance that one or all of those things would get back to their mother, who sees nothing wrong with asking Neil about Myra, or looking into Myra's drawers, or using her own words against her. Then her plans would be betrayed, and there'd be a scene right then, and she probably would not be able to leave until her mother calmed down, which might be the spring or even next summer. If it were next summer, she might have to come back to Belmar all over again.

At dinner Al rips a slice of rye to sop gravy and shakes his head. Already his hair is so gray. He is still a young man. His lips are liver-brown and flat. He looks like the health has been drained out of him in exchange for hard work. Your son is no good, he says. A no good boy.

Neil is jabbing chicken with a finger. He looks up and yells Bang, bang.

Al, stop this in front of my sister, Esther says.

Oh, let him, Rose says. Just because he'll probably never get a son he picks on mine.

Now you listen, Al says. You get away with everything. All because what happened with that baby. We walk on eggshells around you. Yes we do.

Myra watches her father shut his eyes against all this talk. All of you, he says, stop this nonsense.

So? Al says, still talking. If that hadn't of happened, would you let this boy take so much advantage?

Oh for crying out loud, her mother says. Tears are already webbing her dark lashes. Al, if you weren't married to my own sister, I'd call the police to have them take you away and lock you up.

Where Neil goes when these things happen Myra does not know. He has gotten up and slipped away somewhere. She'll find him tonight. She has always wanted him to know that she is not like them and he is not like them. Somehow when their parents got together in Niagara or Longbranch or wherever they made their children, a mix was made that was different from either one of them. Sturdy, different children. But how different, he'd ask her and she wouldn't know what to answer.

She leaves her aunt and her uncle and her parents scrapping over their chicken and goes out into the Belmar night, the salty air, the clammy sky. Tonight the boardwalk band is playing Tommy Dorsey, though slower, and there are couples moving in a loose mass. Out beyond them the beach is empty except for the teenagers drinking beer by the surf. The sand will cool her feet. Her feet hurt from wearing her pumps instead of the ruined espadrilles. She walks along the boardwalk to Roman Avenue. There the cars go two-way, no stop lights. They rush past each other's flanks.

It's a busy night. She hears honking. Must be carousers blocking traffic again. She stands at the corner and looks down the avenue to see what the honking is for. Horns sound to-gether and come apart.

There is a boy in the street, riding his bicycle down the mid-dle of the road, on the center line between traffic. He's riding in the narrow gap between all those cars coming and going. Just one boy being reckless and causing all this commotion. He comes toward her and Myra can see that his face is pale and wild under the streetlamp. It's Neil, holding up the cars of good families coming back from Snyder's Fish and Grill, from True's Steakhouse down the way. Drivers swerve away from the center and yell. He doesn't seem to hear them. He rides his bike down the line.

You come back here, Myra wants to yell in a voice all filled up. She wants to get off the corner and run over to him, yank him by the arm and pull him out of the street. He's turning around as the cars lurch away from the middle of the road. He heads in the other direction, so swiftly it looks as if his bike has left the ground. Myra watches him until he's hidden between the cars, tests her pumps and knows she could never chase anything in them. And knows she could never catch up to him now.

WORK

10:30 at night (dishes washed, pot roast in the amber refrigerator dish) you got your second wind, went back into the studio, sat in your chair (white chair, smudges retouched with titanium white) and opened the clamshell trays of pigment (the trays from a salad bar as the career girls pushed, the pigments your pyramids). Flicked on the special lamp of true daylight, cast your eyes on last night's work (too heavy, that line of gray). Picked up the flat size 6, swabbed its broad tip through oily cobalt. Walked a line of that blue next to that field of dark green. Delicious, wasn't it, the sound of paint rolling its edge across the canvas, bristles whispering into cotton. Outside in the street's brash lights, people rushed home after dinners out, cabs barked and lunged for fares. A half hour, an hour you doted on your rectangles, golden sections of 8, 5, 3, the stalwart assembly of related but not similar colors (as you always pointed out): cobalt, flake gray, cerulean, prussian, ultramarine. You felt a twinge paring down that block of dark green, that dwindling tint that never mixed the same. By its formula in your pigment book you'd written, *not quite*. The midnight streets turned leather in the drizzle, traffic thinned out. In your studio the canvas leaned back against the easel for a long conversation. Your husband called goodnight, got in bed for an old movie, soon the hap-happy of a dance number tapped on the walls. The lamp of true daylight buzzed loyally behind you. Crowded now, that green was causing trouble, a murky hole in the field. You only live once, you thought, and took up a dab of winsor blue, painted over the green, restored order to the world.

TRY

Cloudy early Friday, the flood recedes and takes with it little Hiram, Lula, Lila and Hank. Its force tears them right out of the ground, leaves a barren plain. What's left inside Fawn is a brown and empty balloon. And so on Saturday Fawn and Harlan go to Plum Beach, where an extremely scrawny raccoon scavenges the tidal flats, looking for trash to eat. Apples and watermelons float near the shore, last night's offerings to the ancestors.

Every night the Pakistanis come to Plum Beach and cast fruit into the dirty sea. The Pakistanis throw fruit and the West Indians barbecue and the Russians jog and do calisthenics along the shore. The beach is haunted by the smell of rotting horseshoe crabs, some up so high by the grass that Fawn wonders what their last thought was—head for high ground? Were they killed by the condo sewage dumped along the coast? Invisible toxins?

In the soupy shallows floats the barbecue detritus, cartilage feathering off bones. Their dogs, who galloped down the beach, are now orbiting back but they haven't spotted the raccoon, a fact the raccoon seems to understand as it scampers away with its belly tucked up, a glance behind. This is an unusual raccoon, possibly an aberration of a raccoon, a second-rate specimen—no neat markings of silver gray and rich brown, no booties or clown mask, just a wire-haired smudge with beady eyes, shuffle-rushing away, backbone hunched.

We'll try again, Harlan says. It sounds almost like a question, but he often states things in questions so Fawn's not entirely sure what to say.

So she doesn't say.

This is not a windy, beachy beach. This is a dull-aired, garbagey beach. They watch the raccoon catch its breath near an implant of grass in the sand. They walk the walk of not talking. Fawn holds an apple in her hand that she was going to eat in some attempt to nourish herself but it seems preposterous now, and the apple suddenly weighs about fifteen pounds, an apple made of rock.

I don't know, she says.

Then here comes the cell phone's cha-cha rattling down the beach, and there on the beach is her mother all the way from the airport in Des Moines, breathlessly recounting the latest fuckup on her father's part. They are on their way to a cousins' reunion, one of those things her mother just thought they had to do.

Hi, says Fawn. How are you? How's your weekend been so far?

She means, Can you ask, how am I? Can I tell you? Instead her Mom says, Well, here we are in Michigan, I mean Iowa, what's the difference. And you know what? He forgot his ID. Every time we go somewhere I say, Do you have your ID? Because they won't even let you on the plane these days without your ID at least, and we have to make the connection. And I had to tell everyone who he is, which was hard because he would not say a word, so I said, who else could he be but my husband? He's not the type to blow up a plane. And they seemed to believe us. And then I just got off with FedEx who said Memphis has a sorting problem. So that's something else.

A sorting problem, Fawn says. It reminds her of Hiram, Lula, Lila, Hank. She had been imagining pushing all four of them, burdened to the hilt with all that sticky, pinkcheeked joy. This is not really fun, listening to this latest condemnation of her father, who seems to want to sabotage things these days with his own amazing omissions.

Fawn stops walking and crouches down in the mangy sand and so Harlan stops too, because ever since they first found out about Hiram, Lula and the others, they wanted to be linked at the hip. But since yesterday morning it is a different kind of link, it is a skipped breath they both skip, a way they both narrow their eyes and stare at red lights until they bloody the air.

Mom, you're just going for the weekend. It can't be impossible to figure this out.

Did I say? Did I say? I'm just trying to explain this. But what I meant was, even if we asked you to go and get the ID it won't even get there, it would get stuck with the sorters in Memphis, and oh here's somebody, got to go.

Walking the walk of not wanting to talk about the grand talker in her life. Whew, says Fawn.

I know, Harlan says. They hold hands. The apple pulls her other arm all the way down to the ground. It drags its own path, a bum leg.

Dad will call now, she says, watching a man with a barrel chest jog while doing bicep curls with soda cans. And then Dad does. She says, Good job, Dad.

I know, he says, muzak wheedling behind him. But we're getting on the plane so I guess it didn't work. It's a pain in the neck.

He means flying with her mother. Going anywhere. It could be going from uptown to downtown, it would still be a pain in the neck.

There is the twinge of something like responsibility, like a tug to be there, an urge she's learned over the years to resist, even if she has no excuse. But this time, it wasn't even an excuse, it was something real, it made her feel almost remarkable that way.

I really couldn't go, she says.

All the same, says her father.

I wasn't supposed to fly in my condition, she says. She had imagined the air pressure of the cabin sucking it all out of her, all those expensive treatments whooshing out and then slithering down the seat cushion and getting lost among someone's knapsack and magazine bag under a nearby seat, all four of them blinking and tiny and lost among the navy blue.

Whatever the reason, her father says, disconnectedly.

That was the reason, she says. But it's useless to try to explain. They are just too old. If they don't explain something themselves, then no explanation exists.

The debris collects into little groups in some places on the water. A seagull lands on the flank of an old melon and pecks into the green skin. Fawn wishes there were some kind of sunshine so it would feel like the beach. That the water was blue or at least green instead of dirt colored, that it had little waves at least. Everything is so still, like a bathtub someone forgot to empty.

We have forms to fill out, her Dad says, so give my regards to Broadway.

Harlan gives her that poor-you look as she closes the phone and so she explains the latest. They are on their way to see cousins they never see, there will be nonstop retelling around the table about this singular lost ID thing until the cousins are completely alarmed and her father's shoulders are shrugging up above his head and Mom will still keep telling the same story, Fawn says, each time from a different angle, as if somewhere there's a clear solution and she'll hit it eventually.

I'm sorry, Harlan says.

It is annoying the way Harlan often says sorry when he has nothing to do with something. Yesterday Harlan said he was so sorry. But Fawn does not want to be annoyed by Harlan or ever criticize him in any way or ever henpeck or otherwise scold him ever ever, so she overlooks everything intentionally, everything, even the way he hangs his socks across the straight bar of the floor lamp to dry, so they drip over the arm of the old wing chair, and she tells herself, it doesn't matter, I don't care, I don't care, it doesn't matter.

You don't have to be sorry, Harlan, she says, but with no edge or sharpness. She says it gently, an arm around his shoulders. She has polished her responses to the slightly shiny smoothness of pebbles at the gem show, which she once saw women buy little sacks of by the droves—so ridiculous, these lonely women thinking pebbles could keep them company just because the sign said Love Rocks and the little sacks were handknit.

The jogger with the soda cans runs past them, pumping and sweating. All this sweating. Fawn says to Harlan, Dad once told me that there is no real reason to reproduce if you don't have to. That you might as well just live your life.

Well, Harlan says. And so he forgets his ID rather than saying he doesn't want to go to Iowa.

I don't know about trying again, Fawn says now.

I know, Harlan says.

Their dogs are still arcing up and down the beach. The yellow dog who might be part-Lab is in the lead as usual, the little brown dog who might be part roast beef chubbles along a distance behind. There is no pretense to them. They are what they are.

Still the apple weighs down Fawn's arm. Harlan points out the raccoon as it resurfaces among the tufts, something pink and lumpy hanging from its mouth. Fawn's cell phone rings again as they continue walking and not talking, and Fawn presses *Silence* and does not open it. And then she hands Harlan the apple. Do you want this? I really don't.

He says, Thanks, I do. He knuckles his fingers around it. Wings it into the sea.

FACTORY

In the factory on the hill, something has happened. At first it's scattered, the boxes fight to stay closed. The goldfish bowl becomes filled with green. The machinery begins to leak oil, scrapes against itself, chugging against the seizing parts. The workshirts fight for shoulders. All they've ever wanted is to settle easy and somewhat above the world, to feel warmth in their threads and continue their intended purpose.

Though an open window it must have come: the interloper, the nucleus-eater, rank devourer of everything in sight. The great pumps freeze up and a chill settles over the ductwork. The bins, usually full with new parts, shining and waiting to meet the world, sit fallow. The metal arms hang limp in their housings.

Still the managers keep the records, speak into their little gadgets, tracking the successes, then the setbacks. They suggest a discussion of new tactics, they suggest the assembly of a stronger force, they suggest that they import a mechanic from far away, but the mechanic is on vacation, the stronger force is in development, and meanwhile rust has attacked the holding tanks, acid is leaching out. And so they start the pep talks, outlining their strategies with the letter-numbers B12 and F and P, they have meetings to discuss the false starts, but they are getting headaches and people are calling their names, and they agree on a brief shutdown, on retooling and starting again just as soon as the weather clears, just as soon.

It is a sunny day when the ball bearings of the central turbine freeze in their sockets and the smell is bilious, smoke fills the failing room. The managers shake their heads, look at their silver watches, put their hands back in their pockets and quietly turn away. They have done all they could and they bid the factory good luck, perhaps it can face the elements by itself, perhaps it just needs a rest, they say. They load themselves into cars and drive out to the seashore—at a table by the water they will crack open lobsters, they will relax over wine, they are sure they will find the answer then. And at the last minute, over soufflé, they order a last group of workers, tell them, you'll find the key by the door, just let yourselves in. They sign an order, they go back to dessert.

And the factory stands alone on the hill. The windows squint against the coming rain. But first there is a great gust of wind, and it blows open the doors of the place, it blows the stacks of cardboard boxes out into the courtyard, and they land everywhere and on top of each other in great disarray. And then there are the rains, waves of windy, driving, umbrella-cracking rain, and the cardboard loses all its strength and melts all over itself, corrugation turns to pulp. And then in the office the sheaves of managerial plans surf the turbulent air and land splayed and forgotten in corners, soaking up oil, becoming debris. And the fish left in the office in the bowl gives a gasp and turns white, and then sinks down to that thin layer of blue gravel at the bottom, waving its tail against its last dreams: free current, clear water.

And the shirts hang cold and empty on the hooks, waiting for the workers, didn't someone say they were arriving tomorrow? Tomorrow? And then there they are, the last group of workers, but they don't even want to get off the bus, and they walk in and roam the factory unable to find any tools or even parts to work on. And meanwhile the noise of the sooty birds roosting in all corners overhead is deafening, the rafters are a rookery of confusion, and so instead the workers go to lunch. And sit unhungry in the courtyard among the mash of former boxes, looking back at the factory, its broken windows, its sagging roof, and then simply walk off the job. It's not that we don't care, they telegraph the managers. Stop. It's just that you sent us into a mess. Stop. There won't be any assembling anything here, will there. Stop. Anyone can see that.

Inside the great hall, the floor fills with rocks and the birds peck, peck, make nests in the rafters and lay their eggs. It is a wonderful open place for birds. And the days and nights go by, and the stars waltz overhead, and the sky is blue every single day, and the water in the fishbowl begins to dry up until it vanishes into the air and all the green turns to dust. And there is the goldfish, dried up mid-dream. Still facing the direction of that faraway current. And the birds, sharp and relentless and glossy from breeding, find the goldfish and devour it, leaving a little patch of blue gravel at the bottom of the bowl. The gravel is a saturated, concentrated blue, a bright and thirsty blue created somewhere in a factory where blue really mattered, where they really got it right. And the blue gravel looks through the tattered roof of the factory, and gazes up happily at its long lost mother, the loving sky.

I'M NOT QUITE FINISHED YET

I knew when she brought all those apples to the apartment there would be trouble. She cut into one and apple smell filled the entire place. I was all the way in the bedroom, I was still hooked up, but I smelled that rotten cores on the ground smell.

I called out, "Those are rotten. Throw them out. I can't stand that smell."

She called back, "But they're fresh, they're not rotten at all. Maybe your sense of smell is off."

"It doesn't matter if my sense of smell is off or not," I said. "This is my house. You can't come in here with apples that smell rotten and just expect me to endure it. I have enough to put up with."

Fortunately I convinced her that the point was they smelled terrible to me. But she said, "Just so you know they actually aren't rotten, and don't actually smell bad."

A button presser, that one. And she got mine. My voice, by then, was a high, dry wail. Does that make sense? A high, dry wail. Babies, newborns, their cries sound all wet. Not mine. It was more like a rattle, sandpaper—frankly there were saliva issues, something I had never even given a moment's thought. The things we take for granted are astounding, really.

And I said, "Don't fight with me and I'm not asking." And I did not like all the emotions inside me, but they were like minnows swarming, flashing and flipping around all the time. Sometimes I'd dream and there they'd still be, like I was looking down into this churning, silver pool. And then in the dream there would be this moment: I would be looking into the pool and suddenly I would realize I was falling, I was going to fall into it, this silver, churning pool, and then I'd wake up. That infernal contraption on the pole would be beeping again, and then there was everything that required. That was a whole other story.

But I am not supposed to be remembering that. According to the doorman at the revolving door here, another over-familiar type, we let go of all wordly concerns upon entering. "Entering what?" I said, looking up at the frame surrounding this revolving door, a masterpiece of neo-Gothic pomp with all that wrought iron and overdecoration, the swollen ovolo-astragal moldings, everything dark and heavy, the glass heavy, all the proportions heavy. But then there is no floor, no walls—just this door and the frame around it. "And what kind of place is this?" I said. I am not one to just blindly accept. You lose money that way, for one. And long ago they used to say things like, "You should be married by now, what are you going to do if you can't find a husband?" And I'd just tell them to mind their own business. And I'd use the g-word. They were so ridiculous, all of them. And yet people honored them and sobbed at their headstones as if they'd been decent people all their lives.

But of course as I'm thinking about all this, there's the doorman still after me to just go through. And the frame around this door is enormous, and even the door is enormous, you can't imagine how you're going to push through, and everything is so fusty. It would make more sense if there was a theater behind this kind of door, and gargoyles jutting from every windowsill.

Now that's something I remember: shrinking away from the facade at the Chrysler Building because up there were those creatures eyeing me, ready to swoop down and snatch me up. Horrifying, I would call this revolving doorway's design, if you could call it design. It is worse than neo-Gothic. It's sort of a neo-mess. Plunked onto the crest of the archway is what looks like a former clock, a giant block of a face with an iron spike for a peak. But at some point someone took the hands out. Vandals, I suppose.

"Just go through," the doorman said again, as I hesitated. "No one's coming out, if that's what you're worried about."

"I'm not worried about that," I told him. I explained to him, the way I have to explain to everyone, that it's just that my shoes are loose so I have to take my time. He smiled at me, a rather patronizing smile I thought, which is when I noticed that even though he was dressed like a fairytale doorman— those epaulets and gold braid on navy, really quite gaudy, his uniform—that in his face at least he looked like one of those pompous intellectuals who used to divorce their wives in order to marry their graduate students. That big bushy beard, those little pig eyes, the mama's-boy flush to his round cheeks. Now that I am in this state, I suppose I can say whatever I want. I can think it, anyway. And now he was looking down at my feet. "Loose shoes," he said. "I've never heard that one before. But take your time. In fact," he added, kind of laughing at his own joke, "take your time and keep it."

"You are not funny," I told him. Why pretend?

Once, long, long, long ago, when some women still wore gloves and hats everywhere they went, I bumped into a woman coming in a revolving door as I was trying to go out. It was at a department store. It's this revolving door that makes me think of it. I must have been shopping for shoes, or perhaps a spring coat. In those days you had a spring coat and a winter coat, and a raincoat, and an evening coat. There wasn't all this shapeless parka nonsense you see grownups traipsing around in these days.

But this woman, she was so pushy. One of those pushy women who won't wait, trying to force her way in the door as I was going out. It is so rude to barge in somewhere without letting someone out first. It is inexcusable. You are supposed to let them out first. So I said, "Please wait your turn," and I kept going. I held my ground.

But she didn't back up. Foolish or what, she didn't budge. And it happened so fast, and somehow, I knocked her over.

Then she was on the ground, an old lady, a grey bony heap.

And all the blood! She'd cut her head. She had this tiny head. All these people stood around, looking at me like I was some kind of terrible person. It was awful. But it wasn't my fault, I know it wasn't. You have to let people out first, then go in. That's the rule, or we'd all be crashing into each other every minute.

Isn't that a worldly concern I have supposedly let go of? Do you have to make a list and then get it authorized? What's the system here? I would like to ask someone. They have a phone bank with house phones, but if it's anything like anywhere else they'll put me on hold for hours. I suppose that isn't really an issue anymore, but I'd just as soon find the beach.

They have cubicles here. You sit and wait for an intake specialist, and it is just like a stupid hospital, like a lab where they have untrained people doing the sticking, which was always so annoying. "You'll feel a pinch," they'd say, and then they'd be troweling underneath your skin. At least there is no music, none of that piped-in mindlessness that is supposed to be soothing. Who thinks of these things? There is only a stack of papers on each desk, maybe bills, maybe statements.

If they try to charge me for this I will protest. "I never asked to come here," I'll tell them. And this business about letting go is a crock. Here I am sitting here, luckily I can put my feet up on the chair across from me to help the circulation, and I am thinking, I can't help it, I am wondering, *Who is going to do the bills?* I had everything organized. I had all the paperwork in blue files. I had notes everywhere, only blue, and they were coded. I was so proud of coming up with that code myself. But I never told anyone what it all meant. And now what?

Sometimes, so far, I can see down. It feels like down. It could be up or to one side or another for all I know, everything seems so upside-whichaway. But it feels like down. And I get a glimpse of the dining room table, and the kitchen. There are paper towels all over the place, they are like fallen leaves all over the floor. And someone, I won't say who, has now taken to leaving fruit around in bowls. More apples. Which I can still smell. They are miles away from the refrigerator. And there is rot, unrefrigerated decay, browning pulp.

That was months ago, the apple thing, probably in the fall, since she tended to make seasons into some kind of food thing, always going on and on about seasonal foods like it was some kind of new invention. And I remember it was chilly then. Every once in a while someone would forget to keep the windows closed and that cold air would come rushing in bearing who knows what. But my sense of time is beginning to evaporate: the past, the present, just kind of swirling together. And who knows what you'd call a future here: the Long Float?

I tell the intake guy, this nondescript guy with nice eyes, maybe Irish, that I still smell the apples. "It is not a good smell," I explain. I ask him, "Isn't that a worldly concern? Why am I still thinking about the mistakes on the bank statement?"

He says, "Go see that one over there and she'll help you sort it all out."

"That one over there to which you are referring is an apparition in white gauze with a cape," I say to him.

"Wings," he says offhandedly as he checks off some boxes next to my name.

"I don't believe in wings," I tell him. "The whole concept is a ridiculously antique idea designed to convince foolish people to give up all their money to churches."

He says, "And we have a pamphlet for that." He reaches up into the cubby and hands me a piece of paper folded in thirds, just like an old-fashioned mimeographed copy. Remember the purple letters, the typewriter look to it all, the smudges? You'd roll the drum by hand—*gu-guh, gu-guh*—and the pages had that inky smell. And even though the paper is folded in thirds, it's just one unbroken block of text all over the page. Again, I am sensing a lack of good management, but I read it anyway:

> The concept of the angel may be baroque but is not a construct. It is within us, something ingrained in us, the hypothalamus of our collective emotional aesthetic regarding loss, what Pablo Cohen called our Angelaschammerschaften-aufwiedersehen (L.V. 1921), in which we give wings to that which we can no longer access, or possess, let alone understand—a metaphorical adaptation, if you will. Consider within that context the possibility that haloes were not meant to convey upward essence, but in a covert sense act to "weigh down" the uprisen, suggesting the weight of bronze and gold (please refer to

your copy of Janson's *History of Art*, page 57, the original 1962 printing, the one you have in your bookcase on the third shelf from the top, not the new, revised edition you bought in the museum bookstore the day before the blizzard they'd predicted, when you realized the children were going to be stuck in the house and might wind up drawing all over the color plates).

The intake man points up at his own head, and I see now that it's crowned with a halo, one of those heavy gilded things, like a cut-out halo for a school play. He leans forward confidentially and whispers, "The truth is, I just can't get it off. I've tried everything."

"And who the hell is Pablo Cohen?" I want to know.

He scratches at his halo thing. He has a nice profile, this one. He has a bit of a Portuguese fisherman thing going on, some extra meat over the bridge of his nose. It would be interesting to sketch if I were twenty-one and back in art school.

"If I have to wear one of those things," I say, "I'd prefer white gold, something unlike bronze and certainly not garish, something in keeping with my own religion, which is modernism."

I've got his attention.

"Instead of organized religion," I say, "they should have had organized architecture, organized art. We would have had fewer wars. Have you heard of modernism? It does not just live in museums. Modernism is a decision. It is a choice. I always asked the nurses for blue or gray socks instead of beige. They were always telling me, 'But lady, people like earth tones.' 'Don't lady me,' I'd say, 'and please bring gray socks.' People have this idea about earth tones."

To my surprise he nods. He crooks a hand. He says, "I *hate* earth tones."

One remembers little hooks. Snags on little moments. My neighbor's daughter was once stung by a wasp and there was nothing we could do about it, she just stood in the street and cried her head off. That was when I realized I could live in a town no longer, and who cares about all those trees.

And the flavored coffee that overweening proprietor served us once at a B&B in Tucson. Imagine drinking coffee all fussed up with some fruity scent for breakfast, let alone for any meal at all. "Some things are just not *done*," I tried to explain to her. "Coffee has enough of a flavor without berries or mint. It has its own integrity."

"Would you prefer I make some hazelnut?" was all she could think to say.

She was so confused. Just dim. To say she suffered from a failure of imagination would be to admit she had an imagination. But since this was Arizona, I suppose I should have cut her a little slack. Really, the things people think are elegant. For instance, florals, these garish awful patterns, which if you are sensitive visually and stare at too long, and if there is that olive-and-scarlet thing going on, which some unwitting middling designer decided was classic, and so there it is, on everything from curtains to toilet seats—

So far, fortunately, there is no chintz here.

I've made a few mistakes. It's probably not a good idea to mix art and food, for instance, though I was always trying. Once, during my time in that town, I made a dinner entirely of blue foods. I used food coloring. Why not? That was before the dangers of chemicals were known, before all sorts of things. And truthfully, I don't know if all those warnings did any good. I mean look at me. But the blue food thing: I served duck with blueberry sauce. The sauce came out a very, very dark, ashy navy. I served red cabbage, dyed blue. The boiled potatoes came out more like lavender. I was careful to use foods whose natural colors were already compatible with the color blue. Or else the dye would have just turned them black. You couldn't have served oranges, for instance, or sweet potatoes, which, with blue added, would just come out the color of mud. So many people don't consider the color wheel when they do things.

The blue food was meant to be like an adventure, something fun, a little domestic conceptual thing to break up the monotony of all those neat streets and houses. I even dyed the milk blue. It came out a lovely shade of periwinkle. But the kids looked down into their milk and said, "Yuck." I was so surprised. They wouldn't touch any of it, not even the applesauce, my only non-blue item, which I'd managed to tint a velvety forest green. I guess I had been thinking it would be good to brighten up the blue with another color, but nothing too garish or unsettling or unbalancing.

"No way," the kids said. I wasn't going to argue with them. It was meant to be fun.

"I thought you'd like it," I said to them. "I thought that you'd think it would be like drinking the sky."

"It looks like it's from outer space," they said. "Can we have pizza?"

So maybe they were a little young for a sensibility. There was still time back then. At least they had imagination.

Of course I didn't even bother pulling out the blue cake. The cake, I'd made a white one from a mix and then I used so much blue dye that it came out ultramarine. The frosting was chocolate, but I dyed that black. So it would have scared the kids right out of the house. I just waited until they'd gone to sleep, and then I quietly ate it. I sat in the dining room, looking out the window at the blue moon. The house was silent, a blissful, thick kind of silence. Sitting on the pure white plate, the cake looked magnificent. No one else ever knew.

PHOTO: NINA SCHULTZ-TERNER

Jana Martin grew up in New Jersey, Boston, and New York City, graduated from Oberlin College, and received an M.F.A. from the University of Arizona. Her story "Hope" (included in this collection) won a *Glimmer Train* Short Story Award for New Writers. Jana's stories have also appeared in *Five Points, Spork, Willow Springs, Yeti,* and other journals; her nonfiction has been published in the *Village Voice, Marie Claire,* and *Cosmopolitan.* Jana is a regular contributor to *Yeti* and to sporkpress.com, which hosts her fiction column, *is mink hollow.* She lives in Woodstock, New York, where in her spare time she is learning search and rescue with her dog Lee.